*Excerpt*

Nate couldn't help but reflect in the wink since he'd spun toward that inviting whimper—for a man who sure liked an awful lot of unplanned things today, why should he be surprised at how very much he *adored* the fetching sight of the stunner before him?

"Oh," escaped from him, as he readied himself to apologize.

But the stunner appeared to be in shock. Was grabbing at her throat.

"Miss?" Forgetting his attire—or lack of it—in a wave of concern, he stepped forward. "Are you all right?"

"Qu—quite!" She fanned the air in front of her face. "Simply strangled on some spit. 'Tis all. Don't mind me."

But her face was poppy red, eyes flushed, and—

And when he saw where her gaze had landed and remained, he realized why.

*To the devil with me, I'm standing here practically naked!*

And in front of a lady.

"Damn me. Oh, hell, didn't mean—"

*To gawp back like a lad? Curse about like a dolt?*

"To swear!" he yelled at himself, partly embarrassed. Mostly intrigued.

Other women had never rendered him pudding-headed. *Why does this one strike me dumb?*

"Ah, forgive me. I— Um..." His mind cast about for an explanation, his tongue a way to say it without further cursing—or floundering.

"My shirt," he said inanely, pointing past her shoulder, toward the wheelbarrow now sporting both shirt and jacket, "seam split. Damn near tore... Uh, I vow—" He'd vow he typically didn't blubber about. Nor curse in front of ladies.

What was so difficult about explaining that he'd ripped a shoulder seam? That the torn sleeve had slid straight off the end of his fingers, once he'd pulled at the unraveled threads, leaving the remaining portion of the shirt gaping indecently?

*Oh, aye, and if she hasn't gone running by then, you might very well tell her your trousers are so painfully snug that any second now you have been expecting them to split nigh in two.*

characters are fictional creations; any resemblance to actual persons is unintentional and coincidental.

Proofread by Judy Zweifel at Judy's Proofreading. Cover by Erin Dameron-Hill at EDHProfessionals.

At Literary Madness, our goal is to create a book free of typos. If you notice anything amiss, please let us know. litmadness@ yahoo.com

# CONTENTS

# LADY IMPOSTER

STEAMY SCANDALS
BOOK TWO

## LARISSA LYONS

She has no money, no connections, nothing that can tempt him.

— JANE AUSTEN, *PRIDE AND PREJUDICE*

# PROLOGUE: MEET APPLICANT TWENTY-FIVE

WINTER 1814

THE WIND WHIPPED at his back, fluttering the edges of his unbuttoned coat. Naval Captain Nathaniel A. Oliver's booted feet met the patch of turned earth, darker than that around it, but he dared not take the few sparse steps closer—the ones that would bring him face-to-slate with his wife's tombstone for the first time.

Dry-eyed, he could read it well enough from here.

*Ellen Elizabeth Oliver*
*Devoted mother. Beloved wife.*
*December 12, 1783 – March 30, 1814*

Was she? Devoted to their children, until some

wasting illness snatched first her vivacity, then her very life, aye.

But beloved?

By him? The rotten scoundrel too young and naive to see the burden his life at sea would put on an even younger and equally naive female.

Ages twenty-three and seventeen when they met. Her a pleasant, biddable miss. Him? In alt over his recent promotion to commander, eager for a bride, both for himself but also to impress his senior officers. Had to show his maturity, that he was ready to command his own ship.

A scant few months later they wed, with their first daughter born less than a year later while he was away. No surprise, that, for he was always away, leaving Ellen to manage on her own.

He hoped the angels held her now. Could in some miraculous way make up for all the nights he never did.

And, now that she was gone, all the years he never would.

Dark clouds scudded across the sun, ushered in by the increasing winds. Blinking against the sting, Nate's gaze flicked over the three matching tombstones to the right, only slightly more weathered than Ellen's, though the trio had been standing a decade and a half longer. Her parents and older brother, all three gone the winter of '01. Just months shy of him meeting Ellen and her older sister, Sarah.

Ellen had been the youngest. Pampered and shielded from how harsh survival could be. Nate had been too, despite his years first at school and the handful at sea. Both blinded by youth and passion. Nate too eager over the thought of having his very own woman to see how desperate the two women—girls, really—had been to find homes. Futures beyond working at the local tavern for tups and tips.

At the time, Nate barely had eyes for anything beyond his dreams of His Majesty's Navy and his young bride, spinning air castles right along with her through their frequent letters after they said their vows and he sailed right off, his head full of trumpery about heroics and the glories of war, his heart content at the thought of a sweet, amiable wife awaiting his return, and his conscience buffeted from agonizing over the look of longing in her eyes as he waved goodbye by the significant portion of his pay he sent home.

Even as his youthful passion for her waned, with distance and time, his heart grew to cherish the friendship that developed between them, their bond of affection deepening throughout the years thanks to their lengthy letters.

And his expectations of glorious war and returning home a hero?

Napoleon and the cannon blasts that took out first his ship, and then his good friend's leg—and almost Luke's life—did away with those posthaste.

Not to mention the more recent unholy skirmish that riddled Nate's skin and destroyed Tucker's ears. Damn war. His mottled skin seemed the least of it, when his two fellow officers lost a lot more than a few inches of smooth flesh. Between Tuck's hearing and Luke's leg? Made Nate appreciate being able to stand on his two, ocean-longing feet and hear the mournful cry of the wind whistling between the tombstones.

Those experiences and others had left a man in their wake. One who matured beyond idolizing war or fantasizing about perfection or passion long since gone.

Left a man who loved his growing family—thanks to brief shore leave home and a fertile female waiting with arms raised—even if, at times, he guiltily suspected he loved the sea more than her eager embrace.

Left a man who grieved to learn his wife had sickened, but who savored her every letter, every scrawled word even more.

And when she died? She left behind three adorable daughters and one navy man who mourned the loss of his best friend. The loss of their joint innocence.

And who guiltily resented her absence and how it, *and* the end of the war, brought his feet firmly to shore, when he still, even now, longed for the sea more than anything...

1

## THE MARRIAGE SCHEMER



Mid Spring 1815

Esteemed solicitor Mr. Bamber Hastings might present himself as a grumbler in public, but that was only because years of dealing with officious prigs such as Horace Letheridge had crusted his exterior.

Inside, he was sweet as a sugared comfit, or so his dear Margaret claimed as she rubbed the tension from his shoulders after he returned home from hours at his office in Duffield, Derbyshire.

"Aye, Maggie Mae," he told her, his voice rough with utter fatigue, "right there, my love. That's the spot."

In truth, Bamber had thought to retire well over a year ago, to spend his remaining mornings on this earth sleeping in, his remaining afternoons taking his great-grandsons fishing, and his remaining evenings by the fire, watching Margaret knit while they both took pleasure in the soothing, relaxing conversations shared between two people with nothing more pressing on their plates than being with each other.

But when the always dour and oft despicable Horace Letheridge up and died, finally, leaving his sweetly innocent and young *sixth* wife a widow, Bamber and Margaret had jointly agreed he would keep his shop doors open a mite longer. Just a sufficient length to assist the new widow through her grief (not that he expected her to have any, but one never knew).

Fact was, he'd hoped to see deserving Lady Juliet Letheridge quickly settled in a better situation. Then Bamber would be free to blithely continue on his way toward retirement. Instead, the intrepid widow was met with one catastrophe, and one creditor, after another. Assailed by assorted disasters plaguing the unentailed properties she remained in control of. And Letheridge's heir to everything else (the title, entailed properties and vast coffers), a distant nephew with a home and life in Bath, refused to spare a farthing to help her.

So when Lady Letheridge came to his office, accompanied by her companion, spouting fantastical notions of *advertising* for a rich spouse, instead of dissuading her as he would have anyone else, or if the fish—and his great-grandchildren, of course—hadn't been calling his name so loudly, he considered the preposterous notion against his better judgment...

Contemplated the rotten-as-they-came man her father had forced her to wed...

Cast about for a convincing reason why he should stomp out the notion posthaste...

And couldn't.

Couldn't dampen the hope brimming in her eyes or destroy the heartfelt, if nonsensical, notion of giving the young widow a chance to have a say in her future. One she had not been granted, he gathered, in the choice of Horace Letheridge, as a bridegroom some years prior.

If Lady Letheridge wanted to choose her husband this time, why, by Zeus, Bamber resolved to do everything within his power to help. Trying not to feel guilty about his other motivator, the ones with gills. For he truly did desire to see the young lady safely and securely settled, for her own sake.

After all, he'd chosen Margaret when he was but a green lad of twenty and they'd been merrily married for going on fifty-seven years now, which was certainly a feat to be prideful over. He must have *some* talent for satisfactory spousal selection, Bamber reasoned.

During the process of composing the (scandalous, to be sure) advertisement and deciding upon requirements to be verified during the process, he'd come to know both the lady and her companion, Miss Olivia Hales, on a more personal level, beyond the silent, seen-and-not-heard way he'd known them previously, in the presence of Letheridge. The cranky codger had always demanded Bamber present himself in person at his estate, deeming it "beneath a peer" to journey to a tradesman's place of business.

Lord Letheridge had also liked lording his station over his wife and her companion, requiring their presence at these meetings as well, though the under-valued womenfolk had been forbidden to speak. (Thanks to his dear Maggie Mae, Bamber knew full well to value those of the gentler, and more gently reared, sex. It always bothered him the way men such as Horace Letheridge derided and disrespected anyone not exactly like themselves—buffoons with ballocks for brains.)

As to the current scheme he was reluctantly facili-tating—*Aye, fishies, I'll be coming your way soon.*—Bamber already had a candidate in mind for Leth's young widow; he only had to pray the man read the papers and was interested, or desperate, enough not to let pride keep him from applying for the position of purchased husband.

"Knotted up tighter than twine, tonight, Bams," his Maggie Mae said, thumbs digging in hard enough to make him grunt. "I thought ye were ready to be releasing your work and worries, not heaping more upon your head, aye?"

Whereupon he shared the normally confidential goings-on at his town office, needing the wisdom of his trusted wife.

"So if all goes according to my wishes," Bamber told Margaret after she'd reduced his muscles to mash and had taken up her knitting in the chair alongside his, finishing his tale, "we shall see the advertisement in several of next week's newspapers, that Mr. Tanner fellow will apply and satisfy the requirements, sweep Lady Letheridge off her feet and me onto my rump with my fishing line sunk deep."

The needles paused in their rhythmic *click-clacking* and she shot him an evaluating look from beneath her lashes. "Then what is it that concerns ye, Bamber? Why the furrow deep between your brows?"

"'Tis the fate of the companion that keeps troubling me."

"Miss Hales?"

"Aye. When we finished the composing today, all three satisfied—if a bit embarrassed—with our efforts, and she bowed her head as though with equal portions of relief and regret, it came to me. She reminds me of Nell." His never-married, newly deceased, sweetheart-of-a-spinster sister. The one who, in the dark corners where others couldn't see, he'd glimpsed a sad, unsatisfied expression. "I don't think Miss Hales has given up, not completely, but I do believe she's close."

"Given up," Margaret queried with care, "on life, ye mean?"

"Nothing of the sort," he rushed to assure her, reaching over to pat her shoulder. "Given up on finding happiness for herself, to my way of thinking."

As always, Margaret read his mind. "A man, you mean? One for herself? Ye think Miss Hales has abandoned all hope?"

"Aye."

"'Tis not your job to help her, now is it? It's the

other one, the lady, ye have been so worried about. Or so I thought."

He'd been worried over both women as the weeks had eclipsed since Horace Letheridge's demise, dire situations filling the female's days and flooding their cellar, with both of them remaining resolute about finding a way to provide for the tenants inhabiting the lands first Letheridge and then his horrid heir woefully neglected. "Mayhap not my job, but my duty. To both of them, I'm thinking." Bamber frowned, reaching for his seldom-smoked pipe. "Of course, the simplest thing would be to just do nothing..."

"Think ye might regret that more than causing a possible result that goes awry?"

"Aye. Never have I shied away from taking action because something might not be easy."

"Then find them each a husband," Margaret said as though nothing were simpler. "How difficult can it be?"

"In Duffield?" The small village didn't exactly claim substantial traffic. "Pshht." His lips fluttered with derision as he tapped tobacco into his pipe and reached for the taper. "Other than the two annual cattle fairs, ours is not a hamlet brimming with marriageable men lurking around every tree stump, sprouting forth from sunbeams, not quality ones."

He thought of the quiet, somewhat stoic, slightly plump Miss Hales with the sunny smile and hair. "It's not as if she has a large dowry to offer and entice." After a couple hearty puffs, he worried the stem of his pipe with his teeth. "I don't know, Margaret... I truly do not."

With a creak of chair and bones, his dear wife stood. Her lips met his weathered cheek a second before her parting words greeted his ear. "You will find a way, Bams, you always do."

Now, several hours since his cherished Maggie Mae had retired, he sat at the kitchen table contemplating the quandary, tapping more tobacco into his pipe (and waving his hand to clear the air) as his restless mind wouldn't let him rest.

Not until he'd solved the dilemma.

What to do with Miss Hales? Or for her?

How to see her happily situated, so he could start baiting hooks and hooking dinner?

She seemed a reluctant spinster with that familiar longing he'd seen on his dear sister's face as she beheld the ever-growing families of their siblings.

A look he'd caught adorning Miss Hales' expression more than once as the three of them had jawed out the details of the advertisement's wording and the procedures he'd follow with any applicants, all of them working to shield Lady Letheridge's identity.

It was a look that said she too wanted a friend and lover.

After all, had it not been Miss Hales' idea that they include the last, "all-important" reference? The one she said they likely needed given her friend's sufferings in the bedchamber?

Then, once voiced, had it not also been her who insisted most stringently 'twas nothing more than a flippant notion? One she'd as soon they all forgot had ever left her lips?

Ahhh, too late by half—for once uttered, the Lady Juliet (who by now had bid him not call her "Letheridge" if he could help it) latched on to the concept like a starving cat's claws into a fat mouse. "Of a certainty!" she exclaimed. "Wivy, you're positively brilliant."

"Positively mad, you mean," Miss Hales had protested, leaning forward to emphasize her point as her complexion took on the hue of a ripe tomato. "Juliet, you absolutely cannot require such a thing, much less put it in print. I was jesting, not serious. This scheme of yours is already outrageous enough without adding—"

"*Enough.* It is perfect and shall be included. No more complaints, Wivy, please. Mr. Hastings, take up your pen."

The lady had spoken. And, if more than a trifle reluctantly at first, Bamber acceded to the women's wishes.

If part of finding the former Lady Letheridge a suitable spouse meant the man had bedroom expertise to go with his blunt, who was Bamber to argue? So in went that last part—specifying the required references—worded just as Miss Hales had quipped in the first place: *Also have obtained three personal characters, including one from an inamorata stating, with no amount of equivocation, prowess pertaining to performing duties of an intimate nature.*

Who, just who, was he to find for the female in

question? For unlike her charge, Olivia Hales did not possess several estates comprised of superior lands—and inferior abodes that sat upon them—to offer a rich man in lieu of a monetary dowry. Neither had she the refined, lithesome appearance currently in full vogue with the gentry and peers. Nay, hers was a buxom, lush figure—fine to be sure—but add to that, she was a wee bit past the first blush of youth which might cause some common churls to overlook the hearty beauty staring right at them.

She wasn't yet thirty, he was sure, a year or three shy in fact, but though both women had composure and courage (they had to, to even conceive of, much less *propose* such a scheme), the younger Juliet exhibited a streak of determination he thought perhaps life, or possibly years *protecting* Juliet, had sapped from Miss Hales.

The more he'd gotten to know her, the more he'd realized she accepted her fate, had become resigned to life as an unwed spinster without any hope of *more*. Took it as her due or some such nonsense.

Bah. He had seventy-plus years on this earth, most all of them lived within four miles of his birthplace—just on the other side of Duffield. He ought to be able to find one worthy lass a weddable, beddable man.

Casting his mind for an appropriate alternative, someone he might know he could cozen an introduction with, someone who would value the uncommon sense and subtle but pithy witticisms she bandied about when she thought no one could hear her, Bamber threw a glance heavenward. "A little help, if you please, sir—or madam," he added quickly, always willing to accept the unexpected when petitioning for Divine Assistance. "Anything would be most appreciated. If you can see your way to—"

*Ahhhh.*

A gruff sigh of pure contentment drifted through him when the candle flame did a little *poof* and went out, not a single draft about the place, and him just trimming the wick not a quarter hour past.

As the tiny waft of spent flame wound its way upward, through the gentle haze of tobacco smoke he and his pipe had created, Bamber sat back and smiled. "Ah. All right, then. You shall see it's tended to. Thank you."

<hr>

THREE WEEKS LATER, as he sifted his way through the applications—the pile heftier than he'd ever anticipated—Bamber was still pondering the problem, as the Almighty had yet to provide sufficiently for his peace of mind.

"Miss Hales," he muttered, pausing to ink his pen after writing down the name of the twenty-third applicant he'd decided sufficiently met Lady Juliet's criteria, even though after reading through the references, Bamber thought the man overly vain and prone to conceit. "Why must you pose such a conundrum?

"And you, Mr. Irritating Tanner, why must you be

so stubborn?" For the one applicant Bamber had prayed would apply had yet to do so…

It wasn't until the following day, when he finished slogging through the applications that he experienced a calmness in his soul. A peacefulness that filled his heart, along with his head.

And this only after cackling like an old hen, when he finally opened and studied the last two parcels. One from young Mr. Tanner (thank you, Lord); the other causing such mirth that Bamber's sides hurt and eyes still watered, even now, more than an hour after perusing the most entertaining application yet.

*Ah, yes,* he thought with no small amount of glee, as he painstakingly wrote in…

24. Zeus Tanner
25. Nathaniel Oliver

This last name had a star, for Bamber would be contacting applicant twenty-five directly, given the more incongruent details of his thoroughly entertaining application packet.

*Aye, now,* he thought again.

The bait *was* sufficient and the fish have bit.

*Now to reel them in.*

2

# INTERVIEWS BEGIN—AND END

LATE SPRING 1815

A REMOTE ESTATE, 17 MILES OUTSIDE OF DUFFIELD

"THAT BITCH!"

The coarse, masculine shout came from beyond the crypt of a room where Nathaniel Oliver had been entombed in all morning, following on the heels of other, similar and derogative complaints about their mysterious hostess.

Nate welcomed the harsh complaint because it took his mind off his sore armpits and likely bruised ballocks.

"Tricking me like that!" the unseen griper continued, from the far end of the narrow corridor. "I hope she gets the pox from the flea-ridden old cuff she finally picks!"

"You'll not be speakin' such," another decisively male voice barked back, "not with womenfolk about, and not in my 'earing!"

The commotion brought both Nate and the other man in the dungeonesque room—both still waiting for their audience with the infamous Lady Scandal—to their feet.

"What in blazes...?" Mr. Tanner—the other remaining fellow—muttered. Though clean-shaven, unlike himself, he was every bit as muscular as Nate. Earlier, the other man had confided his sincere suit toward the unknown female they were here to meet; unlike Nate, who was simply here to apologize and leave, having no idea the effort would require hours of waiting and garment-inflicted pain.

Curiosity overriding patience, they made their way around the huge, stone-topped table that had, until dwindling to the two of them, contained upwards of a dozen men since morning.

Stale smoke hung heavily in the dim air, partly from the meager candles attempting to illuminate the room, but mostly from the heavy smokers that had been in their midst until being summoned, and then discarded, one by complaining one... Though none quite as vehemently as the man they now watched the servant, introduced as Jacks, forcefully escort past the room with a brief nod in their direction.

"Up for following?" his companion asked.

"Definitely." Nate reached across the scarred table that had likely seen more than one human sacrifice given its monstrous size and decrepit condition—or so the two of them had traded quips over—and reluctantly retrieved his new jacket.

Reluctant because he'd as soon leave it there to rot.

Nate shrugged into the horrid garment with a groan, making haste down the hallway and into the empty kitchens where his barely sated stomach flinched inward at the faint hint of lemon and yeast, of butter and goodness and something recently baked.

Scents of home. Hearth. Family.

Inanely, a vision of his three daughters, their slim hands wrist deep in flour, dark hair pulled back in long braids, laughing over the work bench as they readied treats for the oven brimmed in his mind, filled the empty kitchen with emotion that tugged at his hungry middle even more than the idea of food. Shaking off the crazed illusion, Nate swallowed down the imagined taste of a buttery lemon biscuit. Rid his mouth of the idea of *home*.

He'd best not long for things he had no business expecting. Not a scandalous land-rich wife, nor his family happily ensconced in this decaying yet beckoning abode.

Back in the boarded-up mausoleum, upon the sacrificial table they'd been centered around, Nate had hauled out the rest of the rations his sister, Susanna, had sent him off with. Used to sharing whatever was to be had aboard ship, it was nothing to dole out the remainder between the men. He'd soon seen, however, how a hearty portion of sliced roast, gravied vegetables, and bread to sop—and top—it off intended for one didn't stretch very far among five hungry men.

Nate just hoped the stable boy who had taken his horse this morning had grass and hay to spare for Blueberry. Or was it Bluebonnet? More pet than people carrier, the mare he'd borrowed from his brother-in-law wasn't used to going hungry—or carrying a man the forty-plus miles they'd traveled since yesterday.

Too bad he didn't feel comfortable pausing to scrounge up a carrot or other treat for Mistress Blue-bell as he hurried through the kitchen. Alas, he hadn't time to waste to inspect the food stores, not when the place was protected by a ham-fisted foot-man. One who had no compunction about delivering swift justice.

So Nate followed his ears and marched himself straight on outside into the overrun garden where the burly footman, who seemed more like a prize fighter than a servant, first deflected, and then delivered more than one sound punch directed at the buffoon who continued to bluster and tirade, insulting Lady Scandal and all who "did the bitch's bidding".

*What am I doing here?*

Watching a one-sided fistfight and hoping the "gentleman" labeled previously as applicant twenty-three loses only because most of his jawing throughout the dark, smoke-congested hours consisted of how he couldn't wait to bed the "Lady Wench" they were all here to win, how anyone desperate—"and beef-witted" enough—to advertise for a rich husband had to be so god-dog ugly, she'd be thankful for any primed cock that came her way.

Accurate or asinine, it didn't matter; all morning Nate had yearned to slog the man's puffy lips and slimy smile.

*Another one to the gut ought to do it*, Nate silently cheered the prize-fighting footman when Twenty-Three only whined more complaints, deriding the lady further using language so foul even a hardened navy man such as himself winced.

*What am I doing? Encouraging a servant to wallop a weak excuse of a man?*

*Oh, aye, that you are and enjoying every minute of it*, his brain or conscience confirmed—he never knew which—but during the quiet hours of watch, Nate had become adept at pattering with himself.

Enjoying? Was he really...

The exchanges with Tanner (applicant twenty-four), once it had been reduced to the two of them, and the fight, certainly. He enjoyed both. But the rest of it?

Traveling here under pretense?

Feeling both guilty and flattered by all that had transpired to bring him to this point?

Delaying yet again his sincere search for a home for himself and his girls?

And worst of all—

Wearing brand-new clothes his sister had tailored for the occasion and waited until his departure to rummage his bag and tug out what he'd rolled and packed only to replace them with her offerings. "We need you looking your best when you meet your future wife, Nathaniel. Do we not?"

Now *those*—his clothes—he wasn't enjoying a shred.

He'd left way too early that morning to see if the small village of Duffield had any available ready-mades; mercantiles didn't open in the dark hours. And 'twas too late to don his traveling clothes as they'd gotten muddied beyond wear when he'd stopped the day before to help a family with a broken carriage wheel. So he'd worn what was available to him and regretted it ever since.

Susanna might have a heart of gold and exemplary sewing skills, but she certainly couldn't claim any talent when it came to fitting him. Especially not after nearly two decades' absence. Barely stifling a groan, he shrugged his shoulders for the seven hundredth time since he'd donned the ill-fitting shirt and jacket that morning, hoping to alleviate the sharp pressure where the constricting sleeves cut into his armpits and threatened to cut off circulation.

He might have been a lean lad of thirteen when he last saw his toddling sister on a daily basis, but hard work and a hard life had filled him out and hardened his muscles—and sometimes his outlook, he feared—until that lanky lad had been replaced by solid man.

The fight wound down, the crude roister taking his leave with his tail—and broken walking stick—tucked firmly between his legs, thanks to Jacks' fighting prowess. Who—he and Tanner had just learned—in addition to escorting the unwelcome bounder out, was also here to escort the next applicant up.

Up, to the second level where the interviews were taking place.

Loath to be banished back to the stuffy, smoky crypt where he'd idled away his morning hours and then some, needing desperately to feel the sun upon his face, the wind caressing his cheeks, to be moving his body in some manner before the utter stillness drove him to Bedlam, Nate inquired whether he could take a simple stroll around the garden while he awaited his summons upstairs.

Permission was kindly granted and the other two men returned inside, with Jacks admonishing Tanner to watch his step up the stairs, something about their rickety nature.

Nate laughed at that. "Rickety doesn't begin to describe it."

He ran his gaze over the faltering façade of the once grand home, now decayed almost beyond the point of repair, that nevertheless still brimmed with character. No matter, the stately manor house would never be his. *You're not here to vie for the lady's hand.*

Nay, he wasn't, but speaking of hands, his left one had started to tingle again. "Damn jacket."

So he took it off, slinging it first over his shoulder, then upon an overturned, rusted-through wheelbarrow.

He rolled up his shirt sleeves, evaluating the overgrown garden, seeking a trail or walking path but instead spying a rusted hoe propped against a low stone wall, nearly half the rocks crumbled or missing.

After tripping over some weeds run amok which he rather thought were supposed to be herbs on his way to retrieve the hoe—see? three months ashore and he still wasn't steady on his now land-locked feet —Nate shook out his right leg, hoping in vain to rearrange how the sister-sewn trousers fit as well.

Damn crotch seam had been sawing into him all blasted day.

3

ONE MAN'S SEWN DISASTER IS
ONE WOMAN'S PURE DELIGHT

"Did I not tell you from the beginning this idea of yours was fraught?" Oliva "Wivy" Hales inhaled so deeply her lungs strained over the stampeding lurch of her heart. "Good riddance," she practically spat toward the doorway of the sadly cheerful sitting room where she'd interviewed wealthy applicants all day. Where Jacks, their footman/butler/*Jacks*-of-all-trades had just bodily hauled out the most recent candidate.

"Glory be, he almost struck you," Juliet breathed behind her.

*I know.* "Twenty-three's temper far exceeded his qualifications. Be thankful you discovered it so swiftly."

"I am. But fraught or not, prior desperation calls for bold measures now." Hidden behind Olivia's brightly attired form seated at the desk in full view, secreted beyond the embroidered screen, her charge and friend Juliet (whispered about far and wide now, the scandalous *Lady Scandal* whose identity they did all they could to shield) gave a weary sigh. "Stay the course, dear friend. There are but two remaining per Mr. Hastings' meticulous list."

Mr. Hastings, the wizened solicitor Letheridge had used for years and Juliet hired upon her aged spouse's demise to help her advertise for another—before her selfish sire could marry her off yet again without giving her any say.

"Correct, you are," Olivia told her from memory, "only two more. A Mr. Tanner, nothing else stated, and a recently retired navy man, a—"

"Retired?" Juliet's gusty snort came through the screen. "After Horrid Horace"—her disgustingly departed—"I was aiming for someone younger. Not infirm."

Olivia laughed. "You peagoose. Navy men start young. Thirteen or fourteen is not out of the realm. Tack on fifteen or twenty years' service and I doubt he's a cane-dependent doddler. But even if he is, a *good* man is all we seek for you."

"One with bulging pockets, lest you forget."

"True." Olivia thumbed through the stack of papers upon her desk. Finding today's list of applicants sent round by Mr. Hastings, she quickly dipped her quill in the ink and heartily crossed through the ill-mannered scrubs they'd interviewed so far. She needed to give the solicitor a strong reprimand the next time they crossed paths. How could he condone such sorry applicants and condemn Juliet and herself to entertain them?

Sweet, innocent Juliet was land rich and pocket poor, thanks to inheriting all her husband's unentailed properties but none of his funds. When fiery flames destroyed the favorite and other tragedies rendered a couple others uninhabitable, they had retreated to this run-down, long-ignored estate.

Though the three-story manor house was spacious, everything was old and faded and creaking—her chair reminded her when she shifted. With the kitchen and a very imposing male domain they had dubbed the "study" on the ground floor, with so many of the windows boarded up to avoid taxation, the women spent most of their time on the middle floor, here in this somewhat furnished sitting room, or in their bedchambers above. When the rain allowed, that was.

Despite her calm conviction in front of her charge, a shudder of unease slid heartily through her just as Jacks pounded on the doorframe, announcing their next churl—er, *applicant*.

Hoping for the best, anticipating disappointment, she pasted a pleasant smile across her face. "Welcome, sir."

"Z. J. Tanner, at your service," the tall, formidable man proclaimed the moment the beefy Jacks ushered in their second-to-last candidate and quit the room. The stranger speared her with a hard glare. "I believe we have much to discuss, you and I."

Olivia blinked and sat up a little straighter, stiffening her already vertical spine. Well now. Applicant twenty-four certainly wasn't lacking in the confidence department, was he?

Nor was he lacking in the looks department, being solidly built and possessing a head of thick, sandy-colored hair. His piercing blue eyes weren't anything to sniff at either.

But, alas, he seemed disappointed. Gravely so. By her appearance? Or by that of the dilapidated, dingy room they currently occupied?

Did it matter? He wasn't here for her plump, no-nonsense self. And he had the heavy pockets to see this place put to rights, else Mr. Hastings wouldn't have sent him.

She exhaled and braced her palms on the desktop, flashing an even more brilliant smile, arming herself to start the trying process all over again.

Previous interviews had not gone well—evidenced by no less than Juliet's newly casted leg (thanks to applicant number nine's numerous pesky pointers) and Olivia's sorely tried patience (compliments of all the others). After the Broken Bone Calamity last week, the remaining applicants had been rescheduled.

"Mr. Tanner, I do thank you for joining us today," she told him. "I am Olivia Hales, my lady's companion. She has entrusted me with the task of ascertaining your responses to a few questions."

Mr. Tanner scowled, blowing out his obvious frustration on a loud sigh.

Olivia raised one eyebrow, frowning. This certainly didn't bode well, not if Mr. Huffy here was already in a dither—and before she'd posed her first question, much less the rather odd ones she'd learned to save for last.

"I had initially taken you for her ladyship," the man confessed, widening his stance and wiping the pinched look from his countenance.

"You did?" Olivia was delighted by that—after being told by Hairy Horace (Juliet's recently demised boorish chub of a husband) that she resembled a dairy maid with her stupid smile and simple mind— and huge, ponderous teats, the oaf—she welcomed any flattering remark to the contrary, no matter how infrequent they might be. And if the scurrilous excuse for a titled man had thought her simple because she'd occasionally made it a point to spill his snuff on his shirt or his smuggled brandy on his boots and calmly smile over the matter, then so much the better.

Juliet always steamed silently when her wart of a spouse had ordered Olivia about because he was too cheap to staff each of his homes with the proper contingent of servants.

But the toad was dead, her "teats" were safely away from his pudgy-eyed leering and loathsome pawing, and her happy smile was, interviews notwithstanding, real these days.

After the troubles that plagued their earlier inter-viewing efforts—and they were many—they'd decided upon their current scheme: Olivia posed the preliminary in-person questions while Juliet watched, unseen, from the corner. If Olivia didn't approve of the responses, O-U-T he'd go, without ever blinking eyes upon the fair—and desperate—Juliet.

As she ran through the list, and Mr. Tanner answered every usual item put to him as well as the unusual ones, often with lip-curled mockery but always with pert honesty, Olivia began to think mayhap they'd found Juliet's proper match at last.

But when a hiding Juliet loosed a not-very-quiet snort of laughter after one of those honest answers, his eyes narrowed at the screen behind her. He stepped closer, demanding, "Need to begin by asking a few questions of my own, starting with how the blazes a female who lacks the gumption to show her face expects to convince me of her 'readiness to bear my children'? That is part of the bargain, as I recall, and unless you intend to practice immaculate conception right along with the Blessed Virgin, I daresay you will be showing me significantly more than your face before the deed is done!"

"Mr. Tanner!" Olivia's face fired up several degrees at his blatant speech. Her hands fluttered as her tongue floundered for the next question or the proper response. "I—I..."

Juliet came to her rescue with another muffled snort followed by a full-out, hearty laugh. "Wivy, you may leave now. I shall conduct the rest of the interview. I do believe I'd like to be alone with our guest."

Keeping one wary eye on applicant twenty-four, Olivia leaned back toward the screen. "Are you certain?" she whispered. "After the last one..."

The one too free with his threatening fists and vulgar accusations after discovering their ruse.

"Wivy, you must leave," Juliet insisted with quiet dignity as Henry, her gold and white tabby who made himself at home wherever they placed his food bowl, *whooshed* in, slinking quickly past the newcomer to find some snug spot for a nap.

"*Please heed me on this,*" Juliet fairly hissed, sounding quite intent to be alone with this applicant —something she'd not desired with the others. Then louder, voice composed once again, "Olivia, do please tell the remaining gentleman how very appreciative I am he expended himself to such a degree but I will not be able to see him today."

She was so sure of this Tanner fellow, she was dumping out the last one like a used chamber pot without even a meet? "Juliet—"

"I'm afraid I cannot reimburse his travel expenses, but if you will see he's served refreshments before he leaves? Oh! And tell Jacks he may bring in the scones and tea at his convenience."

Olivia shot her a look through the embroidered screen, muttering, "I like this one, but I certainly hope you know what you're doing."

Rising with as much composure as she could, she stepped from behind the desk and walked toward Mr. Tanner. Quietly, so she wouldn't be overheard but with firm emphasis, Olivia told him, "She possesses more brains than sense, my lady does, but it comes with a heart of gold. Be gentle with her."

After emerging into the hallway and instructing a

curious, hovering Jacks to fetch the tray, she pulled the door shut behind her, surprise making her reluctant to release the tarnished knob.

Well. That had been unexpected. Leave her charge and bosom friend alone with a truthful thief? And a formidable, scowling specimen to boot.

*At least he's not a murderer.* Her lips quirked at his recent responses to the questions she'd posed. Nor overly fond of pointers—a boon in his favor to be sure.

Peeling paint marked the stout door she hesitated to move from, the chipped antique white antiqued more by time than design. After it had collapsed off its hinges their first week in residence, Jacks and Jacob, their remaining stable boy (who needed more than one when Juliet no longer owned any horseflesh that required stabling?), had rehung the door to its current non-listing exactness.

The exchange of murmurs reached her from the depths of the sitting room, one deep and just a shade from belligerent. The other carefree. Joyous almost.

Recalling the sincere expression, and the quickly masked vulnerability if she wasn't mistaken, in Mr. Tanner's gaze just before she quit the room convinced her that Juliet was in no danger.

Unlike that lout just prior, the one who'd exhibited no ability to laugh at anything, Olivia sensed Mr. Tanner possessed enough self-assurance and inherent composure that nothing unduly untoward would occur. Pah. Applicant twenty-three. To resort to violence and slurs, and all because the brute took exception to being "duped by two bitches" or so he'd claimed when Juliet had the misfortune to sneeze, giving them both away.

Rude ruffian, assuming he could buy his way into respectability, as though money answered everything.

Give Olivia a man with a ready smile and an appreciation of the absurd, a hard worker not afraid to get his hands dirty and one able to laugh in the process. She'd take that over one with sovereigns to spare any day.

Most days of late, she'd be grateful if only a man would *look* at her and really see her.

It'd been a long, long time since a fellow had paid attention in her direction with something akin to interest lighting his eyes. Companions were paid (or not paid, in her particular case) to blend into the background. To become invisible. Something she'd perhaps accomplished over the years with too much zeal?

Mr. Tanner had gazed at the screen as though he could see beyond it. With hope lighting his expression. And determination.

And that was *before* he'd ever clapped his peepers on the fair Juliet. Aye, her mistress was in good hands at the moment. Safe, strong hands, if she didn't miss her guess.

With a decisive nod, she abandoned her station. Duty called.

Tell the final applicant he wasn't needed? It was a task she dreaded.

To be cast last and now discarded without an

audience? What man would take kindly to such news?

Resolved to see the onerous task over and quickly, Olivia swept down the long hallway, cringing when a bit of wall plaster dusted her dress as Jacks approached, his arms laden with refreshments, and she stepped aside. "Excellent timing."

"This bodes well, do ye not think?" Jacks halted to ask.

"What? That she wanted to be alone with Mr. Tanner? Aye, I do. Tell me, Jacks, is our remaining guest still situated in the study?"

Jacks gave a brief shake of his head. "Asked if 'e could stretch 'is legs a bit when I came for the Tanner gent. Believe 'e's out back, walkin' the garden fer a spell. Maybe tending 'is 'orse in the barn."

What they often called the *barn* was actually a fair-sized stable. Timber walls and a tiled roof that had seen more repairs than the house meant the (non-existent) horses stayed drier than they did. Had the place been a long-ago coaching stop? With the size of the stable and the large courtyard between that and the manor, 'twas feasible to imagine it thus.

"Very well. Carry on."

"You shall see to 'im, then?"

See him off, he meant? "That I will."

Olivia proceeded toward the stairs, thinking, and not for the first time, how this old, neglected home could shine if only someone would devote some tender love and thoughtful care to it.

*Someone such as yourself? As you would as well?*

*What? Thrive with someone's thoughtful care? Tender love? Bah.*

On-the-shelf companions weren't considered marriage material. Far from it. And the sooner she quit contemplating otherwise, the more content she would be.

Upon reaching the landing, she mentally chanted *three, eleven* and *seventeen*. Heading down, three, eleven, seventeen—those were the ricketiest treads, the ones they all took pains to avoid; heading up, they equated to two, eight and sixteen. But down it was...to do the dusty—not quite dirty—deed of doing away with applicant twenty-five.

At the fourth tread—the one with a board nailed solidly over it (to cover the boot-sized hole gouged in the baluster side, compliments of Jacks' heavy foot the day of their arrival), she paused to admire the flocked paper lining the wall. Even greyed in places from its original deep purple hue—still evident where paintings had been sold off, leaving darker squares behind—it had an aged grace she found endearing.

Truth be told, despite its sadly neglected air and propensity toward rot (thanks, she was sure, to the splintered roof tiles and resulting leaks) the old house charmed her.

Especially the gardens.

Though as overgrown as one might expect given the state of the structure they surrounded, the grounds still retained a glimmer of their former sparkle. *Something to appreciate another time, missy, and not when you have an unsavory task to see completed.*

Safely skipping over the last questionable stair, she hopped over a chipped tile in the entry and headed for the massive front door, wrenching it open after only two attempts. Better at weather predictions than any soothsayer or tricksy knee, the ancient wood never failed to swell when rain approached.

The verdant, lush green of a spring in full bloom greeted her, lent a lift to her spirits, and she fairly flew over the flagstone path that circled the old manor, intent on intercepting their errant applicant before he came back inside. Bad news was best broken under a sunny sky, or so her mama had always claimed. Olivia spared a quick glance upward and cringed. Today, a cloudy sky would have to do.

Rounding the second corner, her feet stumbled to an abrupt halt. Her breath hissed inward. Her eyes nearly bugged to Bedfordshire and back.

And her heart? That hurly-burly organ took off like a galloping horse—stealing away with her common sense perhaps?

Because instead of swooning or shying away, instead of yelling loudly for Jacks, Olivia stood, happily, *hungrily* in place. She stood stock-still and she *stared.*

Stunned. Savoring the sumptuous, unexpected sight...the play of muscle across a strong, bare back as applicant twenty-five (for who else could it be?), completely unaware of her presence, wielded a Dutch hoe in one corner of the weed-infested herb garden.

Most notable of all? He was dressed in nothing more than black tall boots and tight black trousers.

Obscenely tight trousers.

Well now.

And to think, Juliet had complained there wasn't anything of value remaining on the grounds.

Olivia begged to differ.

## 4

## YE YOUNG LADY WENCH BECKONS...

<hr>

ASTONISHMENT PINNED Olivia's breath in her chest and time graciously waited for her to gawp her fill. Which she did until her lungs burned as though she'd been fighting a fiery blaze for hours.

Not making even the slightest sound to inform him of her presence, she allowed her tightly held breath to slowly ease out.

She might have been trained to teach proper behavior to young ladies and to exhibit it herself, but she knew enough about life and death, about expectations and disappointments to know opportunity didn't often knock. Especially opportunities for observing and admiring a strong, sweaty man wearing absurdly tight trousers.

So she watched. And her dratted throat betrayed her, making some sort of begging, yearning whimper that had her unexpected treat jerking upright and whirling around.

"Oh!" was all he said, a gruff sound of surprise.

*Oh* was right. Oh great day in the gloomy afternoon, she'd never seen such a handsome man. With his shirt off.

One who stared directly at her, as though *he* liked what he saw as well.

Her.

Well now. Mayhap this wouldn't be such an onerous task after all.

A HALF-STRANGLED moan penetrated Nate's awareness. One with an almost breathy, beckoning quality.

Sheer instinct guiding his actions, he straightened and guiltily swung toward the sound. Guiltily because the last thing he was supposed to be doing today was whacking off weeds at the root in a stranger's overrun herb garden.

The very last, given how he was here on the grounds of this venerable old estate for the express purpose to apologize and nothing more.

He wasn't supposed to like the ramshackle estate he'd been sent to. Wasn't supposed to admire the stately three-story structure, albeit one faltering around the edges from time and neglect (and a few thunderous doses of rainstorms no doubt, evidenced by the lightning-induced crack adorning the garret).

Wasn't supposed to appreciate, even remotely—or

so his rational mind persisted—the wretchedly dark mahogany walls and heavy, scarred furniture crowding the space where he'd been stashed all morning.

But he had, finding the dark room with its boarded windows pathetically snug. Comforting in fact, easily putting him in mind of his below-deck quarters on the ships where he'd served.

If it hadn't been for the stuffy, smoke-filled air—and his yearning to be outside and on his way before the expected deluge hit later this afternoon—he could have patiently waited there longer.

Where he certainly wasn't supposed to develop a rapport with one of his "competitors"—the chap who had gone before him. And most emphatically of all, he wasn't supposed to grow bored at being so inactive and take up the first gardening implement he saw, setting to work ridding himself and recently healed body of accumulated energy, and the garden of its encroaching inhabitants.

But—Nate couldn't help reflect in the wink since he'd spun toward that inviting whimper—for a man who sure liked an awful lot of unplanned things today, why should he be surprised at how very much he *adored* the fetching sight of the stunner before him?

"Oh," escaped from him, as he readied himself to apologize.

But the stunner appeared to be in shock. Was grabbing at her throat.

"Miss?" Forgetting his attire—or lack of it—in a

wave of concern, he stepped forward. "Are you all right?"

"Qu—quite!" She fanned the air in front of her face. "Simply strangled on some spit. 'Tis all. Don't mind me."

But her face was poppy red, eyes flushed, and—

And when he saw where her gaze had landed and remained, he realized why.

*To the devil with me, I'm standing here practically naked!*

And in front of a lady.

"Damn me. Oh, hell, didn't mean—"

*To gawp back like a lad? Curse about like a dolt?*

"To swear!" he yelled at himself, partly embarrassed. Mostly intrigued.

Other women had never rendered him pudding-headed. *Why does this one strike me dumb?*

"Ah, forgive me. I— Um..." His mind cast about for an explanation, his tongue a way to say it without further cursing—or floundering.

"My shirt," he said inanely, pointing past her shoulder, toward the wheelbarrow now sporting both shirt and jacket, "seam split. Damn near tore... Uh, I vow—" He'd vow he typically didn't blubber about. Nor curse in front of ladies.

What was so difficult about explaining that he'd ripped a shoulder seam? That the torn sleeve had slid straight off the end of his fingers, once he'd pulled at the unraveled threads, leaving the remaining portion of the shirt gaping indecently?

*Oh, aye, and if she hasn't gone running by then, you*

*might very well tell her your trousers are so painfully snug that any second now you have been expecting them to split nigh in two. For your arse to be sunlight bound, your ballocks—*

*Stubble it!* Nate ordered his wayward thoughts.

Wearing a soft, lemony-yellow dress—that made his mouth water more than any biscuit in memory—with honey-colored hair pulled over one shoulder in a thick, touchable braid that only renewed the tingling in his fingers, the surprised female beckoned him more than any sight he'd beheld since coming ashore. More than any sight in memory, if truth be told.

She had a woman's ample figure—the square neckline of her dress giving but a hint of the full bounties beneath, the flared hips below the cinched waist of her gown all but inviting his hands to land upon them, to slide up and down, find their home and pull her close so he could—

*What are you doing, man?*

Fantasizing about making love with a woman sturdy enough to take a man's full desires. A woman not frail, but one full of vigor and health, one inciting intense, fiery cravings he'd not thought to experience in this lifetime.

*And you about to bid her goodbye? With nothing more than an apology and explanation? Don't be daft!*

*Stay. Stay and see if the brain behind the beauty binds your interest as well.*

While Nate's inner debate waged, her widened gaze remained locked on him. She hadn't shied away from the sight of his bare chest, not once. For a man who practically had more scars than skin in places, it was a balm to his ego, a comfort to his soul, to see an alluring female staring at him so intently, and with admiration.

A thick mass of grey clouds scudded across the sky, cutting out the direct beam of sunshine he'd been basking in. The sudden shade made him shiver.

*Oh, mate, don't start lying to yourself now. 'Tis not the touch of cooler wind that's making you shiver. 'Tis the heat in her eyes. The look of wonder upon her face.*

"Ahhh…" *Find your tongue, man!* "Just making myself useful. Not used to being so damn—ah, deuced idle."

*Fine way to impress the lady you have come to meet!*

Impress? Where did that come from? He wasn't here to make an impression. He was here to tender an apology.

No time like the present, then.

Using the forks of lightning flashing in the distance as a distraction, he shook off the stupor weighing him in place. He inclined his head in a diffident bow. "My lady. Forgive me, I regret too many years in the company of rowdy seamen has stolen the tact from my speech."

*Don't you mean* thoughts? *As yours are veering in the same direction as that last bounder's? The one who kept crowing about how he couldn't wait to prig the Lady Wench?*

Lady Wench, indeed.

He'd no sooner call her that than contemplate intertwining their naked legs betwixt the sheets—

*Liar!*

Ahem.

Ignoring the unwanted intrusion, Nate stared back at his newest, most unexpected, fascination.

She gazed at him as though enraptured. It was a heady feeling, that. One that almost made him regret the purpose of his presence today. He should state his piece and be on his way.

Aye, that's exactly what he should do.

Already, with the bulk of the day gone, he'd need to stay over in Duffield before setting his borrowed horse on a course for home.

It's what he would do, as soon as he apologized for his appearance—a man never greeted a female in such a state. By the devil, he couldn't even remember his wife of fourteen years seeing his nude torso in daylight.

Taking the hoe's weathered handle in a firm grip to steady himself, he walked toward his abandoned clothing—which just happened to be in the same direction as his captive audience.

"Forgive me, my lady," he said when he skirted past her and reached for his torn shirt, "for greeting you with such abominable taste. 'Tis only that your garden here showed such promise, I hated to see it in such a sorry state." He gave a derisive, self-directed laugh. "Sorry state. Much like myself. Unpardonable, I know—"

His skin sizzled from her continued stare. He

stepped back, propped the hoe against the wall and fumbled for the neck hole—in his distracted state, he couldn't tell the top from the bottom, the way the material had split.

"Not unpardonable. Not if it ripped. I could always mend it for you?"

The unexpected offer, the hesitant tone in her softly pitched query arrested his attention away from his shirt and up to her face. Where her sincere, if embarrassed, expression snared his.

"No, you couldn't," he answered emphatically, tearing his gaze from hers to resume his search. A *lady* mend his shirt? Unheard of! "We just met. Haven't met, actually." His words spun in circles as his hands spiraled around the frayed fabric. "No need for us to meet, not really..." *Not with me about to take my leave.*

*Certainly not with you acting the block-headed gollumpus.*

Where in blazes was the damn opening? "I most humbly beg—"

"Oh, don't apologize," she entreated with a breathy sigh, "not on my account, not when your chest is the most blessed sight I have seen in weeks. Years. In ever, I vow."

*It was?* "It is? In...ever?" He paused in the act of sticking his head through one of the blasted openings —no idea if it was the right one—to make sure he'd heard aright.

And then, as though just realizing exactly what she had said, the fetching beauty slapped palms to heated cheeks, stumbled backward and groaned. "Mercy me. My tongue must be the most wretched thing ever—to say such."

"Nay." One long stride brought Nate within touching distance. He fisted his blighted shirt in his left hand and brought his right up to her face, lightly skimming several fingers where she'd pressed them to her eyes. "Not wretched, not when it utters such welcome compliments."

The slim fingers parted into a V, away from one sparkling olive eye—the color of a briny seaport, which brought about an instant kinship with the outspoken lady.

As he watched, transfixed, the opposite fingers veed as well, then she lowered both hands from her pinkened cheeks.

"Oh?" One pert, blond eyebrow arched, and though her face revealed embarrassment, her voice did not. "So you are most accustomed to having praise heaped upon your countenance? Your chest? Take it as your due, do you?"

# 5

# INTRIGUING, IF MISINFORMED INTRODUCTIONS

OLIVIA WAS HAVING a difficult time not bursting out laughing at his surprised look—or jumping into the well at her brazenness.

Since when did she behave brash and indelicate like a street-side doxy?

A low growl of nearing thunder rocked the ground beneath their feet.

She clenched her hands together—to prevent the traitors from shielding her eyes again, for who in their right, or even wrong, mind would ever want to scrimp on even a second of such a bounty—and drank in the muscled array of perfection before her.

"Certainly not, my lady," he said. "Especially not when scars and nicks, new and old wounds abound."

At the serious tone he employed, she made herself inspect his exposed skin and muscle more thoroughly (for when would she *ever* have such a chance again?), commanded her eyes to look beyond the perfect whole to the imperfect parts.

Four-inch faded line on the right side of his stomach—knife wound.

Circular splotch high up near his shoulder—gunshot, perhaps?

A ragged, oblong patch of skin, crawling up his chest to cover the top of his left shoulder—serious burn if she wasn't mistaken.

None of it marred the exquisite sight of delineated muscle lightly dusted with dark hair, of inviting, strokable pectoral muscles perched beneath tight, circular medallions so very different from her feminine flesh and large nipples.

A hard swallow gulped past her parched throat.

A ripple of movement across his stomach drew her gaze. Where the truly gulp-worthy pair of diagonal muscles led from his firm stomach downward, to the tightly fastened waistband of his trousers, where the fine hair in the center thickened—

"What in blooming bloomers is *that*?" she asked before she thought better of it.

Unwisely, unintentionally, she accompanied her shocked question with a touch, trailing one fingertip from the intriguing narrow band of paler skin and darker hair to the side, toward his hip where angry splotches of ink dotted and spoilt his skin. Where harsh twists of puckered flesh marred the pristine perfection of one side, several inches up toward his underarm and down, disappearing past the tight waist of his trousers.

Placing her entire hand on him, trembling palm to solid, sun-heated skin, she curved her fingers around his side, clenching as though to hold on, to take away pain from what looked to be the freshest of all the injuries and forced her stare from his once-torn flesh up to capture his stormy grey gaze. "What in heaven's—or hell's—name happened to you?"

His supple lips quirked in a slight smile. "Nothing you need fret over, my lady, not anymore. Simply life as a seaman, one that's now behind me."

*My lady.*

Wasn't that several times now he'd called her such? She should correct him. And she would, Olivia promised herself, as soon as she could pry her gaze from his, her fingers from his hot, hard flesh.

"Mr...? Or Captain?"

"Christian name is Nathaniel. Nate to my family." His voice was warm, the look in his slate eyes as they flicked over her face even warmer. The cool color should have chilled; instead, it heated her, trembling toes to tremulous lips. "I will answer to either."

Heavens, how boldly inappropriate, to offer her the use of his name. How very...*intimate.*

Trying not to blink—she didn't want to spoil the strange moment—she dragged a breath into her starving lungs. That's why she felt horribly dizzy, lightheaded enough to swoon: Not breathing. Lack of air.

It couldn't be how *he* looked at her... As though, strangely enough, he found himself drowning in her rapt attention—and made no attempt to swim to shore.

She shrugged off the fanciful notion.

What she couldn't shrug off so easily was how his body felt beneath her touch. Alive? Tantalizing? Captivating.

Aye. All three.

His intense gaze had captured hers all right. Beneath longish hair black as coal and sparsely threaded with silver, brushed straight back from his forehead and not stopping till beyond his nape, beneath equally black brows set in a face weathered by years of wind and sun, he stared back at her with an intensity she'd not before experienced.

She gulped again.

Then lowered her gaze to his mouth. No longer smiling, but gently parted, the lips she longed to taste were surrounded by a finely trimmed beard—not a common sight these days.

No, men combed their Brutus cuts forward, over their brow and oft hiding their foreheads. They shaved above their lips, shaved their chin and most of their cheeks, leaving thick side whiskers to sprout forth in front of their ears. (Olivia and Juliet had joked that ol' Letheridge likely had a family of rodents encamped in his.) Men—

"You smile," he challenged, his mouth still solemnly straight, the light in his eyes curious, his body stationary within the outlandish clutch of her fingers.

Those bold, rebellious fingers flexed, tightened upon his skin.

His breath caught at the action; her stomach dropped past her toes.

But she couldn't move. Couldn't stop gawking. Or groping.

One black eyebrow lifted above a curious grey eye. "Divulge your thoughts?" he invited just as a blast of thunder crashed closer than the last. "So I may share in your smile?"

At that she sobered, dragged her hand away and closed it into a tight fist—to hold in his essence for as long as she could.

Avoiding his strangely compelling gaze, she looked past his shoulder, toward the crumbling chaos from which she'd exited mere moments before.

She pressed her lips together, tried to still their trembling. *Stop this inane fascination right now, Wivy! Correct his "Lady" impression and send the man on his way.*

"Your beard—" The words burst forth. "I like it. Hairy Horace—ahm, a man I used to know—had side whiskers so monstrous, I always imagined a troupe of rodents took up residence on either side of his face."

"Magical or musical?"

The strange question brought her gaze back to his. "What?"

"A magical troupe or a musical one?" When she just continued to stare at him, his lips quirked. "Of mice."

Egad, she comprehended now. "Musical, definitely."

His smile widened. "Because mice are so accomplished at Mozart?"

"Strings, yes. Harpsichord? Not at all. *What are we doing?*" She may have posed the question out loud, but Olivia knew *exactly* what she was doing: slathering over a stranger, behaving in an exceedingly forward manner and not giving a farthing for how brazen or sinful or outrageous.

When Jim went off to war and was lost to her forever, no regret loomed larger than that of no longer having him, alive and well and right beside her. But one that came close, one that continued to haunt her through the lonely years, night after empty night, was the regret they never had expressed their love in the most intimate of physical manners.

Despite her youth and innocence, she had been willing, even eager after a fashion, to experience that ultimate passion with her sweetheart, but Jim— dependable, responsible Jim who didn't want to chance getting her with child—he'd held back, insisting their first time "as man and wife" would be with benefit of a ring and with her in possession of his name.

Pah! What had that lofty aspiration cost her? The *love* of the only man she'd ever desired. The only man who had ever looked upon her with both lust and liking lighting his gaze—

Until now. Until *this* man.

Who stared at her in such a way her belly fluttered, heart palpated and her feet fairly levitated off the overgrown ground. She stamped them in place, trying to jolt some sense back into her squirish body, fool that it was. "Silly beetleheads, that's what we're being," she told her shuffling feet, fighting a losing battle to forget that glow in his eyes—the one that sent her insides spinning. "What we're doing. Acting like betwattled little chaw bacons."

"I disagree." He said it so confidently her feet stilled, belly fluttered faster, as she left off targeting her toes and braved his gaze again. "Disagree most heartily."

"Oh?" She used her best governess voice. "If not foolish, then what might you term it?"

"Getting acquainted?" he suggested, tongue firmly in cheek.

"Over your scars and battle wounds, and my harp-strumming mice?"

"Can you think of a better way to get to know another person?"

"Hmm…" Olivia thought hard, she really did. She thought diligently, piously even. But all she could think of was *How might he kiss? What would his gently curved pectoral muscles feel like beneath my palms? His lips upon mine? His hair sifting through my fingers?*

What she said was, "I'm certain there must be a hundred other, more suitable topics people tackle when first meeting." She grappled for a litany and was pleased with herself when she came up with several. "Favorite foods, favorite colors. Preferred books, music. Exchanging religious beliefs, family traditions."

Her satisfied feeling evaporated when the man pursed his lips, then released them on a sigh. "By my count, that's only six. What else might you suggest?"

The stubborn knave. Determined to prove her point, she continued. "How you like to spend your evenings. Your work days, now that they are no longer devoted to the navy. Your days away from work. What manner of leisure you partake of. What games you like. Languages you speak."

The lout had counted each one off on raised fingers. "You're up to twelve."

Now Olivia just felt challenged. "Children. Do you have any? Want any? Large family or small? Siblings? Names? Black sheep? Closet skeletons?" Thinking of the recent interview she'd conducted, she spouted, "What crimes have you committed? Are you fond of dogs? Have you—"

"That's twenty-one," he interrupted. "Have you seventy-nine more?"

"—any? Twenty-*two*! You interrupted before I could finish that last one."

"I—" He bit back a smile. "That I did."

"Most ungentlemanly of you."

"Aye, most."

"But you aren't apologizing? Begging my pardon?"

"Not when bantering with a lovely stranger has brightened this soon-to-be-dreary day more than any other since my feet came ashore?" A gust of wind fluttered the shirt remnants still held tightly in his fist. "Nay, I'm not."

*Lovely?* He truly thought her so, didn't he? That out-of-breath, dizzying sensation swooped through her again.

*Wivy, take hold of yourself! You're here to tell the man to be off, not while away the remaining daylight hours trading quips over his manners—or lack thereof.*

"Mister— Ah, Nathaniel." She really oughtn't derive so much pleasure from simply saying his given name. *Shouldn't be saying it at all.* "Ahem. Though I am loath to be the bearer of bad news—"

"Then do not." He shrugged one strong shoulder, as if to not acknowledge said news was to deny its very existence.

Determined to complete the task she'd been given, she strove to tell him, simply and truthfully. "Were it up to me, I would not be here at all but, but..." Drat! Why did Juliet, at the very least, not grant this one an audience? He was absolutely, abominably *perfect.*

Double drat! Why did the very idea, the thought of her friend even considering the man before her as husband-worthy cause angst to mire her middle?

When she remained silent, reluctant to end this most unusual interlude, he gave her a conspiratorial grin.

"Then we have yet more in common than a love of musical mice," he said as though confiding a secret. "If I am to be honest, neither am I here today by choice."

"You're not?" *He's not!*

Instead of spinning in place, celebrating his admission, she ignored the relief she had no right to feel, the delight bounding through her, and forced herself to continue as the dutiful companion she was. "Well then, that makes things easier, does it not? Though I regret you made the journey for naught, I must tell you that I came downstairs expressly to find you and inform you that your application services are not needed. The interviews are concluded for the day."

"Oh, then you found someone? Settled on the chap who went in earlier? A good sort, I thought. You agreed?"

"Me?" A lilt of nervous laughter escaped.

His body was so close, she could see the light sheen of perspiration glinting on the muscles adorning his magnificent chest, smell the scent of the outdoors upon his skin. The alluring musk of healthy, virile man.

Tempted. She was so frustratingly tempted.

Breath evaporated once again.

As though bidden, she took a step closer. Then quickly two back, her hands fluttering in the air between them as though they would float to that inviting chest and adhere themselves with all due haste. *Would that I could touch him again...just once.*

To fight the urge, Olivia clasped both palms together, tangled her fingers amongst themselves and squeezed, trying to strangle out the urge. What was that he'd said, something about *her* being the one to choose a husband? "Oh no, I never thought this was such a good idea to begin with."

"You didn't? Then 'tis a good thing you forbore acceding to the pressure to follow through."

While she was muddling through that, he stymied her further when he bowed from the waist, in an exaggerated yet still polite way, and waved one arm between—the one not holding his bunched shirt. "And how shall I address you, fair one? Both *Lady Wench* and *Lady Scandal* having no place in this quaint garden."

He straightened, clutched the folds of his torn shirt with both hands. "I can hardly believe we have yet to be formally introduced. My only excuse is that I am able to converse with you with an ease previously foreign to me when it came to ladies of your station. With most females in fact. I fear the ease has made me forgo all sense of propriety."

That outrageous bit of blarney jarred her from the magnificent-chest-induced stupor that held her in thrall. "Difficulty conversing with women? Pah. I think your tongue is sufficiently silver, glibber than gold it is, that I doubt you ever stumble in sallying."

"But I do. For I never lie. Will you grant me the use of your name, my lady? If I'm to leave empty-handed, at least share that much to console me."

"O-Olivia," tumbled out while she debated with herself about correcting his misapprehension that *she* was the lady he'd come to see.

*Oh, what does it matter? In a few moments he shall be gone and you will never see him again.*

*Aye, but 'tis dishonest and—*

A pleased laugh burst from him. "'Tis a right thing you have changed your mind, then, for if I *had* interested you, you would become Olivia Oliver, and that wouldn't do, not at all." Smiling broadly, he nodded to her once. "Nathaniel Adam Oliver is my full moniker, recently of His Majesty's Navy and—"

"Moniker? I cannot claim to have heard that particular term before."

"Means name, something I heard bandied about in London near the docks after making port that last time." His gaze fell to the wheelbarrow where he reached for his folded jacket. Then he nodded toward the patch of garden he'd been working when she first spied him. "I only meant to be a minute but time, it seems, ran away from me. I cannot abide being idle, and after hours cooped up inside, once I was under the sun again, being active stole my wits from my true errand today."

"Your true errand? That's right. If *you* aren't here by choice, then pray, what induced you to come?"

"My overzealous deceitful little brood, that's who —Charity, Faith and Hope. And Susanna, she joined in too."

Hearing the unmistakable affection when he spoke of his "little brood" fired up foreign tentacles of jealousy. Her chest hurt from the pressure of it. *Silly widgeon! You have no cause!*

*Aye, but—*

"But if you have already a harem at home," she accused, refusing to acknowledge the huff in her tone, "whatever are you doing, interviewing for a *wife*?"

He laughed harder. "A harem! No doubt they will love that description. Susanna's seven months pregnant and duck walking all over the place. And Charity—"

"Mr. Oliver! For shame!" Stop ogling his body! He's unavailable to you now that—

As if he was ever available!

She turned to march back inside—he could blame well leave without any offer of refreshments! Several mad steps in, his firm grip on her shoulder halted her retreat.

He slowly turned her to face him.

"What?" she demanded, even as she lifted her shoulder into his touch. *What is wrong with me? Never do I become emotional like this. Never. And never about a man, one I hardly know.*

*Pah!*

A single drop of rain plunked on her forehead. She ignored it, stared hard at his grinning face, and then frowned, her sternest-possible frown. "Why are you looking at me like that?"

"Because somehow I have made a hash of this whole thing. Susanna—the pregnant waddler—is my sister. And the virtues, my daughters."

*Daughters?*

He nodded as though she'd spoken—which she hadn't. She was too busy being mesmerized by how the bulging raindrops plopped upon his black lashes. Upon his nose. His collarbone. His naked—

"Aye. My daughters." The strong fingers clasping her shoulder flexed, then loosened, trailed down her arm and away but not before leaving a tingling imprint she felt down to the tips of her toenails. "My wife died a little more than a year ago. 'Twas my brood's idea to see me married off." He gave a gentle smile. "To someone bold and courageous as Lady Scandal. So you see, I wouldn't be here at all if not for them."

He was a widower. One with motherless daughters. And a caring sister. Olivia's ire and heart melted at the realization. "And I wouldn't have just made a complete cake of myself had we become acquainted through proper channels first."

"Proper channels? Your list, you mean? The one with approved topics?"

"Aye, all one hundred of them."

"But alas," he countered, "at only twenty-two, you have a far, far piece to go, do you not? And though I still have apologies to make, I am thinking you must earn them first."

"*Earn* them?" Her voice pitched high on that.

"Certainly." He rocked back on his heels, looking entirely too comfortable and too confident for a man nude above the waist. "Finish your list and I shall finish my explanation."

Willing to play along, at least for a bit, she rattled off a few more topics. "Who named your children? And why? Have you any other siblings? Their ages? Yours? Did you like being in the navy? Do you miss it?"

"You're up to twenty-nine," he said encouragingly when she paused for a breath.

Riled now, exhilarated, talking faster and louder with each question she uttered, determined to best him even if she ran out of ideas—or air—doing it, she kept going. "What about pets? Have you any? Do you like cats? What about rabbits? What's—"

"Sure," he interrupted, "roasted and with carrots."

"—your favorite holiday? Did your wounds force you from the navy? Do you have a favorite season? How do you kiss? Are you ever going to put"—she sputtered here, coughed, choked back a small bite of air—"on your dratted shirt?"

And with that, her lungs heaved. Chest burned. Lips ached.

Finally finished (knowing she should feel shamed but somehow not), completely out of notions of anything else to discuss, she closed her eyes, dipped her chin. "Applicant twenty-five, what have you done to me?"

"If it's even half of what you have done to me..." The words dragged from him, harsh and hushed, coming from nearby, causing Olivia's head to jerk back up, her eyes to blink open.

He stood too close for propriety. Too far for her liking.

Holding her gaze, he took one deep breath and finished, "Then we are both having an exceptional afternoon."

# 6

# LIGHTNING STRIKES... LUST IGNITES

"INDEED WE ARE." The words Lady Olivia spoke confirmed the nod she gave him.

So they were in agreement it seemed. "A most unusual afternoon, made exceptional by the company."

What now? Tender his planned apology and leave?

*Or tender it and linger?*

Nate decided to test the waters. "One I am reluctant to end quite yet."

Another nod. A solemn blink of those captivating seaport eyes.

Defying propriety, he reached forth and brought his bunched shirt to her cheek, gently blotting several stray raindrops from her flushed skin. "We're both hesitant to end this?" Whatever *this* was between them. "Refreshingly entertaining afternoon."

There. That sounded safe enough. If woefully weak for how the past few minutes had affected him.

"I'm agreed." Her eyes started to twinkle as they followed his arm's retreat and then met his gaze. "Agreed that we both have geese in our garrets."

He honked a loud laugh, pleased as pudding their nonsensical exchanges made perfect sense to her as well.

"Then..." He shook out his jacket and squeezed one arm into its too-tight sleeve. "I shall attire myself posthaste—forsaking this wretched, ripped shirt altogether—and escort you back inside before the promised deluge reaches—"

"Unnecessary. See?" She pointed overhead where meager sunlight broke through along one edge of the sodden, grey mass. "It's moving off already. Let's take a stroll about the grounds, shall we?"

Jacket on—barely—and buttoned, though straining and with his armpits protesting the cruel confinement, he extended one forearm which she took most daintily.

"Thank you, kind sir."

"Think nothing of it, my lady."

And they were off, pretending the ugly storm posed no threat.

Pretending they were both sane and their noggins goose-free.

Pretending a unique bond wasn't strengthening with every second, every step that elapsed.

"I propose..."

"Yes?" he prompted as he guided them through

the neglected garden, avoiding the worst of the weeds, heading closer to the tall structure. He might be willing to dawdle foolishly outside—when he really should be making haste toward Duffield and ultimately home—but he respected the brewing storm enough to seek cover should the need arise.

*Home?* In truth, "home" hardly felt as such, not with Ellen's absence. And not even before then, if he was brutally honest.

Since landing his feet permanently on shore, he'd been considering options, looking at potential places to purchase, but finding fault with every one. *You know 'tis past time you aimed for a spot of fresh scenery for the girls. Something farther from the coast for yourself.* Why live close enough to the ocean to ache for it?

Nay, something new and green and not filled with Ellen's dying breath. That's what he and his muses needed.

"As I have enumerated twenty-nine suitable topics," his enticing companion said, easily summoning his thoughts from the past, "do you not already owe me, at least in part? Could you not recip-rocate with twenty-nine percent of your explanation?"

"Twenty-nine, eh?" He actually thought it was a few more, but somewhere between teasing her about roasted rabbit and hearing her inquire about his kiss, his mental faculties had dropped toward his groin, leaving him more empty-headed than he cared to admit.

"I'm sure 'twas that." Her hand trembled lightly where it rested upon his. Or was that him? "At least."

He placed his other hand firmly atop hers, anchoring her to his side, where the woman just plumb felt *right*. Right height—the top of her head reaching his chin. Right smell—the delicate, rosewater scent emanating from her hair taunting him to take a deeper breath. Right reaction—the electrifying way his entire side lit up at her nearness. "Blazes," he mumbled to himself, "I don't need the storm to strike me down. I think she's done it already."

"Pardon?" Her feet paused and she half turned toward him as they reached a simple flagstone path located just a foot or two beyond the base of the three-story structure that loomed tall and imposing— and protective—beside them.

Cursing his runaway mouth, he turned the rest of the way toward her, released his hold over her hand to fondle the blond braid resting generously over one shoulder. His fingers teased the brown ribbon binding the end; she teased his rapidly disintegrating senses. "My rowdy tongue again," he told her, flicking his gaze from the enticing braid to the inquisitive look she gave him. "Forgive me. That's a difficult bargain you propose, my lady—"

"Stop. You shouldn't— I'm not... I keep meaning to tell you, I'm not—"

He whipped the end of the braid against her lips to stifle the soft-spoken protest. "You *are*. Putting me in a very troubling position, that is. Twenty-nine percent? How is one to calculate that portion of an explanation? Come, give me four more and we shall call it an even third."

"Four and one-third more to be precise," she corrected primly even as her eyes tracked the braid when he lowered it from her mouth, her lips looking flushed. Bitable. Licka—

*Contain yourself, man. Why are you about to blow over naught but a pair of lips? Lips that aren't even stroking your—*

*Lickable, kissable lips,* Nate argued back. Pretty, plump, soft lips. Dewy, now that she'd just moistened them.

Swallowing down a groan, he closed his eyes, crushed the braid in his fist. It might not be long—hours or a day, in fact—since he'd taken himself in hand, enjoyed a quick physical release, but swiving a female? A flesh-and-blood woman?

Not since his wife.

For unlike the many seamen of his acquaintance, Nate hadn't gone tupping in every port, not wanting to poison his prick with pox or the like. He'd heard enough tales of burning piss to keep his pisser to himself. Or his weakening, welcoming wife. But now...

Today—

He gulped and blinked his eyelids against the piercing sun slicing through the heavy clouds. "You give me four; I shall give you the third."

As though aware on some level of how perilous his composure, she spoke in a more subdued manner than she'd used henceforth. "All right. What do you make of our sickening king? Do you have concerns for how his son rules? Do you have a favorite port?

Have you ever been to Egypt? Does our navy even sail there—I confess, geography isn't something I spend time studying." She gave a great sigh, one that gently heaved that impressive bosom he'd tried vainly not to gape over. "Oh, but the pyramids. Always have I longed to see pyramids."

"What about a mummy? Any interest in those?" While he couldn't very well tap his timepiece and wing her off to Egypt, he could certainly arrange a trip to the British Museum in London, escort her to the exhibits, show her—

Excited by the prospect, he snapped his fingers. "You asked about cats earlier. Did you know the Egyptians worshiped them? Mummified them?"

"Noooo." She breathed out a sound of delight. Then spoilt it with a snort. "You're bamming me. Most dreadful of you."

"King's honest truth, I swear. One of my mates who left the navy a while back told me when I saw him last. He had visited the museum and other notable London sites before heading home to Cornwall."

His "I could—" *show you*, got lost when she exclaimed, "Cat mummies? Better not tell Henry. He would likely go into hiding for a year."

*I could show you.*

*I could show you? Your brain topple into your ballocks? You won't see her again after today!*

More's the pity.

Reminded of his true purpose, he reluctantly returned to it. "You have more than earned a third of your explanation, my dear lady." *All of it, man, if you know what's good for you.* He started walking again, placing one foot methodically, precisely—dallying?— in front of the other. "But first, who's Henry?"

She matched his unhurried pace. "Henry the eighth, Beheader of Mice and Vermin. He's Juli—" She cleared her throat. "Ah, a friend's cat."

Ignoring the pangs of abandoning any notion— however ill-conceived—of them, *together*, in London, of showing her the city and its unforgettable sites, he made himself respond in kind—without any hint of seriousness. "I hope he treats his lady friends better than his namesake did."

She laughed as he'd intended. "Most assuredly. Though I do think a certain calico is starting to feel a wee neglected." She leaned in close to whisper. "I hear he's been pawing around a fluffy grey tabby of late."

"The knave."

She bumped her shoulder to his, as though reinforcing their unique camaraderie. "Aye, you understand completely."

He understood too much.

Kinships such as this were rare. A budding bond to be cherished, nurtured...explored. Not summarily discarded.

Nate vowed to himself he'd taste her sweet, laughing lips at least once before he left for home.

With a hard, deep inhale followed by a painful exhale, he forged ahead to the business at hand. "My account is more akin to a confession of sorts. One made easier, I'm realizing, by the knowledge that you have abandoned your quest for a spouse."

"Oh?"

"Aye. Makes my embarrassing tale slightly less so, as I'm armed with the knowledge I shall not be disappointing you."

As they neared the midpoint of the foundation on this side of the manor, she paused to look up at him. "Nearly agog with curiosity am I. Out with it, sir. No more hesitation, floundering, or bargaining nonsense."

"Aye, aye, ma'am. I mean *lady*."

OLIVIA NARROWED her eyes at him.

The strong-jawed, scarred-over retired navy man. Despite the grey streaks in his short beard and longish hair, here was a specimen in prime twig.

And he was bantering about with her?

After he'd interrupted her one true attempt to correct his misunderstanding of her title—or complete lack thereof—the way he dithered about, making her "earn" his explanation...

Preposterous, infuriating, *intriguing* man.

She had half a goose-filled mind to let the misunderstanding stand, but only since he was not here in serious pursuit of a wife. So, she'd be his *lady* for an hour. What could be the harm?

"What?" he asked. "You have a strange look upon your face."

*Aye, thoughts of you put it there.* "Oh, nothing of consequence. I think my garret's gone and flown south for the winter."

"Oh scandalous lady, then let me confound it further. I am here not to seek your hand—though very lovely and worthy I can attest—but solely to tender my apologies. My daughters, with the best of intentions I was assured, forged my application, attempting to gain me an audience with you. I shared all this with Mr. Hastings, but he insisted I tell you. *In person.* And there you have it."

"I am very thankful he did. Insist you come here, that is."

"But 'tis a horrid waste of your time."

*'Tis the delight of my mundane life.*

Bidding him *goodbye* loomed like a bad tooth that was about to be yanked free.

"Nay, a true pleasure it was to come upon you in the gardens." She fanned her hand in front of her aching chest, even as her lips spread in a genuine smile. "I don't think my heart's pounded that ferociously in years. Truly. 'Twas a naughty thrill to come upon a half-dressed man in the abandoned garden. Would you have deprived me of that?"

"Never."

Though she'd kept her tone jovial, he answered with all the solemnity of a minister.

Her hand now fanned in earnest. "Well."

She closed her eyes, striving to break the invisible thread that arced between them. A flash followed by a startling *ka-boom!* had her eyelids flying open. Her mouth uttering a startled yelp and her heart pounding furiously all over again.

Because he wrapped his arms about her and pushed her up against the stone façade. "Damn me, but that was a close strike."

She couldn't breathe. Couldn't answer. Certainly couldn't move. Could only stare at the neatly trimmed beard covering a strong jaw and surrounding quirked lips that looked entirely too appealing.

Like bees honing in on their hive, her fingers fairly buzzed. She lowered her gaze to his chest where she had latched on. One hand against the fine black wool of his jacket. One against heaven.

Heaven in the form of hot, supple skin. Masculine skin. Skin marred by life and war. Manly skin made beautiful by the being who wore it, nicks, burns and all.

A few fine black hairs beckoned her fingers to explore.

Her inborn modesty clucking like a chicken—not to mention society's constraints—bade her to escape.

But it was her experience of love lost, her endless years of empty nights, nights filled with longing and regrets, that commanded her actions. Or inactions, as it were.

Making her choice, she remained right where she was. Where he held her. Stone against her back. Hard, virile man against her front. "So tell me"—she strove to keep her voice steady—"how well did they forge your application? There were several letters of references required. Did your daughters provide those? Did they pass Mr. Hastings' exacting muster?"

His heart thumped solidly beneath one palm—the one touching skin.

The rhythmic beats slowed at her words, then sped up at the realization she was prepared to continue their conversation—in their current positions.

"Oh, ah, *aye*." A hushed intensity filled his words...and the space between them. "With a combination of flying colors and stumbling blocks both."

He shifted one leg, coming impossibly closer. She made a sound of gentle encouragement for him to continue even as her stomach swooped and soared, doing all manner of tricks better suited to a tumbling troupe.

"When it came to stating my financial worth, I gather they were overzealous in their application of zeroes. Once Mr. Hastings ascertained, according to 'my' submitted materials that I was in possession of amounts far exceeding a trillion pounds, and that several times over, he suspected something was amiss. He sent round a note requesting my presence in his office. The girls had, I'm sorry to say—"

But Olivia was already laughing at the image he painted. Laughing and edging the fingers on wool closer to the center of his chest. Closer to skin. "How—how many zeroes might that be?"

"Accurately, it would be eighteen. In my case, I think there were twenty-seven."

The laughter kept flowing. Her stomach dipping and flying. His body easing forward...

"Twenty-seven zeroes?" She ducked her head in a show of respect—actually as an excuse to inhale his manly, outdoor-infused scent—then lifted it to say most primly, "My, oh my, how humble I feel to be in your exalted presence, Your Excessive Richness."

He grinned at her antics, slid one hand from her back, where it'd been lodged, around to her waist where it settled. "You laugh now, but at the time I thought it was a most serious grievance for them to commit."

"How old are they?"

"Old enough to know better. At least two of them are. Charity and Faith are thirteen and nine, respectively. Hope's my baby, at almost five. She's—"

The world flashed. Then twice more. Brilliant sparks of blinding light that built one after the other.

The dual strikes startled a squeak out of her.

The resulting barrage of thunder halted conversation.

So they spoke with their eyes. Their hands.

*What is happening here?* she questioned, trembling within his hold.

*I do not have an inkling but it feels surprisingly good, does it not?* The hand at her waist flexed, tightened. The one still at her back spread wide, rubbed a soothing, seductive path down her spine and back up again.

When the angry echoes quieted, his chest lifted, then fell. "Most egregious of them." His voice deepened, took on a rumbling, dangerous quality reminiscent of the weather. "I told Hastings you needed a man with an authentically large purse, not one with established progeny prone to exaggeration, but—"

"But I would adore your children!"

Then she recalled. "*You*" meant Lady Juliet, with the lands and title in exchange for his money, not her—Plain Olivia Hales, with the...nothing to offer.

When his leg brushed one thigh and his foot slipped between hers, "*If* I were in the market for a spouse," burst from her.

There now. She'd extinguished the flare of excitement in his gaze before it ever had a chance to flame into life. Part of it. But not all, not given the heat generated between them.

"Shame we're not both looking for a leg shackle, as it seems we're in accord," he said.

*In accord about how badly I need your kiss?*

His leg nudged forward until it pushed solidly between the juncture of hers.

She gasped. Dug several nails into his skin and held on. "Mr. Oliver?"

His gaze, which had fixed upon her lips, didn't waver. "Lady Olivia."

Completely without design, her Lowlands flexed toward his strong thigh. Then again.

Scared, thrilled, sensing where this was heading—longer, *lonelier* nights after he left and unwilling to suffer thus all over again, this time as a woman grown with adult urges and yearnings—she ducked her head and pushed at his chest, scooting free, tripping over his foot in her haste. "I cannot!"

*Buwack! Wack-wack! Cluck-cluck-cluck!*

"Oh, Lord." She put one hand on the stone to balance herself, one on her heart to keep it in place.

He took a step back, away. Erased all traces of desire from his expression. "My lady, forgive me." The formality hurt. "For not the first time today, I have behaved most inappropriately. I shall take my leave." He gave a slight bow and turned, heading for the stable.

By the time his muttered "Blighted vow, be damned" reached her ears, she had roused her feet to go after him.

"Mr. Oliver! Wait!"

She raced pell-mell till she was in front of him.

The disappointment on his face convinced her.

Potential regrets aside, she would enjoy this afternoon if it was the last thing she did. Resolved, she took his arm, determined to guide his resistant form toward a part of the grounds they'd yet to cover.

"To the devil with my nerves," she said quite simply, holding tight to his solid forearm and attempting to speak normally—as though she did this sort of thing every day: flirted with strangers, begged for their kiss. "Your daughters. Regardless of the mischief they perpetrate, you treasure them, do you not?"

"Ah..." Although he remained stiffly at her side, seemingly baffled by her sudden reversal, he stopped struggling against her tugs and acquiesced. "Ah...aye, that I do, even more than the most seaworthy of vessels. No matter how many scrapes they get into. I had them compose notes of apology—the two who can write, that is. That's one of the main reasons I came today, to deliver them in person."

"Writing at nine and thirteen? You are to be commended." Olivia knew full well how many females were not granted sufficient education to prepare them for this life.

"Not myself. You may thank their mother for their education. She and my sister saw to that in my absence." A hint of sorrow, perhaps regret, shaded his features as they both jumped when the next loud lightning strike thundered nearby.

"Where are their notes? I would love to pass—" *them on to the real Lady Juliet, the actual recipient.* Her grip firmed on his arm. "Er, read them."

"Damn me, left them and my saddlebag in the tomb."

"The tomb? Visit a lot of crypts, do you? And just when I started to think you were an unremarkable man." Oh, the bounders she spouted!

His posture finally relaxed on a gentle chuckle. "Only the ones lining your drafty manor."

"My manor? Full of skeletons and bad omens, is it?"

"No skeletons. None that I saw. But that room where you stashed us? Not the most pleasant of places, even for someone used to the confines of a ship."

She tried not to notice how warm he was at her

side. How her fingers had taken to petting his muscular forearm beneath the fine wool of his jacket. Tried and failed. Every second with him seemed magical—and hadn't she just promised herself no regrets? So she stroked his wool-covered muscles again and refused to feel any shame. "For that, sir, I tender my humblest apologies. The recent rains, you understand, they have visited upon us not a few troublesome leaks. Your so-called crypt is one of the few furnished, dry rooms remaining."

"And the boarded-over windows that render the space dark and smoky? Your hidden skeletons have an aversion to bright and airy?"

"Not I, but...ye olde purse does. You can thank the window tax for that action." Why only a few of the windows on the upper floors remained usable and let in light.

"Blazes, but I have become waterlogged, having been away so long to forget about that."

No longer was she guiding their steps, nay, they had taken on a life of their own as they circled the extensive manor grounds, the giant structure blocking the bite of wind, buffering the occasional burst of rain.

So they strolled. And chatted. And strolled some more, the minutes eclipsing faster than they should have while at the same time, slowing to a creep so she could savor the buoyant moments of *pretending*. She, *Lady* Olivia, being courted by the most attractive of fellows, one who pursued *her* to wedded bliss and—

And she happened to glance up, spied Henry in

the sitting room window on the second floor, bathing. So either about to nap or just finished nibbling.

Henry, escaping back into the room when drips from the eaves blew over his fur, disrupting his efforts.

*The room with Juliet, the* real *lady hereabouts. Or have you lost all sense—*

Her toe snagged on a paver and she pitched forward. Ground bound, until her companion's swift action jerked her back upright, snugged her against his side. "Take care, now."

His touch across her waist halted the whimsy. *Do not be a ninny, Wiv. Enjoy the now for it is all you will likely ever have.*

She tossed her head and the depressing thoughts aside. "Tell me more of your daughters."

"Brilliant pixies, each and every one." He beamed brighter than the cloud-covered sun. "I realize now how much of their lives I have missed," he added with deep-voiced seriousness, "being gone. Reading about their antics in letters holds not a candle to experiencing them firsthand. Faith, the middle one, she's the quietest, the most like her mother, apt to surprise a laugh out of me no matter the situation."

Listening to the joy in his tone, seeing how his eyes lit up, warmed Olivia all over, made it all too easy to continue the pretense. "Share one with me?" she invited. "One of Faith's surprising laughs."

He bit down on one side of his cheek, as though debating. "All right. But if you take offense, do recall 'twas your suggestion."

Anticipation grew as a hitch tugged in the vicinity of her heart. "Tell me."

He stopped walking, turned to hold her about the waist, loosely within the circle of his arms. "I gather my two oldest hatched the plan to marry us off after overhearing Susanna and her husband talking of your advertisement." Olivia had to clench her back teeth to keep from confessing all—it was never *her* advertisement. "But they had to be inventive when it came to the required reference letters.

"For the first one, Charity pretended a giant cough that left her hoarse for days afterward. When the family physician stopped in to check on her, she pronounced herself cured and asked him whether I was about to die. When he exclaimed nothing of the sort, she requested his assurances in writing— thereby proving my health."

"Brilliant and crafty," Olivia complimented. "She sounds delightful."

"She is. Too smart for my own good. Now on to the personal references. They enlisted Hope, the youngest, who asked my sister, her husband, and two longtime friends to write down what they most liked about me. Susanna realized they were up to something when Charity returned her list, asking her to write it again, this time including my inamorata talents as well."

Imagining the scene, Olivia laughed out loud.

"Susanna went along with it, agreeing to help them gather the requested components only to have Charity post everything before she could offer to.

Knowing my application was erroneously on its way, Susanna came to me with the whole of it. I blew it off as a lark until Hastings wrote, requesting to see me and he shared..."

Over the last few minutes, the temperature had dropped, wind had risen. Was that what brought the ruddy hue to his cheeks above his finely crafted beard?

She somehow found her hand latched to his jacket again, this time the lapel. She fisted the material and gave it a slight tug. "Shared what? Faith's laugh?"

"And then some. Evidently, upon learning from her older sister exactly what my 'inamorata talents' were supposed to be comprised of, Faith penned a letter herself." His slate eyes twinkled at her. "Uh, praising them."

"Oh no, she didn't!" Olivia gasped. "And her only nine?"

"Right. Though Charity already knows more about adult things than I'm sure any parent wants for their child, no matter what their age, the word was new to her and when asked, Susanna carefully explained things in such a way that when Charity relayed the conversation to her younger sister, Faith understood it to mean how I kissed and how a wife might find me appealing when...*naked*."

At his strangled pronunciation of the last word, Olivia released his jacket to slap at the hard muscle of his shoulder. Then again. "Oh, 'tis grand!" She fell forward, laughing harder. "The rest of it! Tell me of her letter."

His arms tightened around her waist, kept her from doubling over. "Going on memory here... Something to the effect of: '*Dear Anonymous Lady~ I have known* ~~Mister Captain~~ *Mr. Oliver my whole life. He is a splendid man and shall make you a splendid husband. He is very strong, with big hugs and splendid kisses. When he takes his clothes off and you meet....*'"

Practically holding her breath, anxious to hear the rest, Olivia prompted, "Meet...? What else? You cannot stop there."

"Damn me." He closed his eyes and tilted his face heavenward. His hands flexed on her back just above her waist.

Feeling decidedly unbalanced, Olivia grazed several fingertips up his neck to lightly scratch his beard. "Mr. Oliver?"

He brought his head down, eyes flashed open and snared hers. "Meet my dangler, by God." His hips flexed toward her then, the motion causing her long skirts to ruffle. "Damn it! Blast me for starting this. Faith wrote how you would like my 'dangler'. Only she called it by name."

Olivia stood there, stunned. Transfixed. Enraptured.

His daughters named his...dangler?

She couldn't stifle her snicker. And he admitted it? Voluntarily shared it? "Named it? Dare I ask...?"

"Gus."

Her joyous laughter bubbled free. "G-Gus?" And

her gaze couldn't help but be drawn downward to that particular area, the one where Gus resided. "They named it...*Gus*?"

"Augustus, to be precise. Something Charity came up with when she was young asking her mother about the differences between boys and girls. Only Faith shortened it in her mistress letter."

Still staring at that particular part of his anatomy, unwilling to admit how very much a naughty part of her wanted to meet dear ol' Gus, to experience for herself those promised big hugs and splendid kisses, the words escaped her lips before she'd thought them through. "I think I'm in love."

But then she did hear them.

And yanked her gaze up from his Gus-region, squarely back to his face. "With—with... In love with..."

He brought one warm hand up to cup her cheek. His thumb stroked over her lips. "In love with... laughter?"

"That will do." When he held her like this, touched her just so? Oh, would that do.

7

# AND THE SEAMS SHALL SPLIT ASUNDER

◦

Lust and laughter—did they go together? Nate hadn't known it could be so.

Several cold raindrops chose that moment to cool the air sizzling between them.

She closed her eyes against the intrusion but didn't otherwise move.

"Lemon," he said musingly, staring over her every feature, trying to memorize each one. To decipher what it was about her, *this* particular woman, that fascinated him so thoroughly. "I smell lemon." That and roses.

The innocent combination did anything-but-innocent things to his body, rousing "Gus" more—much more—than was prudent. Especially considering they were both fully clothed (his torn shirt counted not) and all he touched was the skin of her cheek. The temptation of her lips.

But then more rain fell, intermittent but determined, spitting upon the fair complexion of her forehead, the thick blond of her braid, and he had to touch more. *Had to.*

More storms were coming; he could practically taste them on the air.

"When they're to be had, I rub a quarter of one on my face and neck, and the back of my hands every night," she murmured against his thumb.

"What? Lemons?" Leaving his hand where it melded alongside her face, he wiped the stray drops off with the other. Lightly brushed his fingers across her forehead. Caressed his palm over the top of her hair, down the back. Willed his pesky prick to disinterest and cursed himself—and his dead wife—for laughing along when Charity had first spouted the childish nickname. "Whatever for?"

"Aye." Her closed-eye whisper seduced ol' Gus right back to full interest. Full attention. "My great-aunt insisted 'twould reduce the wretched freckles and keep my face fair, if not fine."

He stopped stroking her hair to take her chin in hand. Eyelids blinked and those luminous, briny beauties stared up at him. "Appears she was partially correct. I don't see any freckles, wretched or otherwise, anywhere upon your fine—make no mistake, *very* fine—"

*Face* got obliterated by the deafening onslaught.

Wind whipped between them in a fury as he squinted against the pelting rain. Coming down loud and hard and straight on top of them, a torrent gushed forth. As did a massive lightning strike that blinded him a full two seconds.

Devil a bit! 'Twas past time safety outweighed seduction.

Popping one button in his haste, he fought to shrug out of his jacket. Once free of the confines, he swung the garment over her head.

"Come on!" he yelled through dripping missiles that hit like ice pellets. The temperature had plummeted in the last few seconds.

*Seconds, man? Are you not paying attention? It's been dropping steadily for half an hour.*

Ignoring the reminder that he wasn't focused on anything but the woman before him, he caught her hand and started off. "We need to get inside. Now."

"The stable!" she shouted back, tugging him the opposite direction. "It's closer."

Fleeing the elements on an exhilarating run, they rounded the nearest corner. Nate headed where she pointed, seeing little more than rain-soaked gloom.

He wasn't sure who lost their footing first.

One moment, exuberance whipped through him as they pounded over patches of puddles and high grass. The next, his right foot went sliding one way while the rest of him slid the other.

They both went down; she to her knees, he to his arse.

Mud ker-*plunked* upon once-clean clothes. Pooled water soaked straight through to skin. And those blasted needle-sharp missiles kept falling.

Colder now. Harder.

"Are you hurt?" he yelled above rioting raindrops.

"Lazy loafer," she laughed, gaining her feet and hauling him to his. "No time to sit on your duff!"

His jacket no longer shielded her, was swinging from her arm.

He narrowed saturated lashes, watched as the pellets bounced off her wet head. "Hail." Dragging her after him, he renewed his advance toward shelter. "Quit dillydallying in the mud, woman!"

"Me?" Stumbling beside him, she matched him stride for stride. "You're the one wearing mud for breeches instead—"

*Cr-aaaa-ck! Boom!*

A flash of lightning startled her silent. Its resulting rumble lent wings to their feet. In seconds, the shadowed entrance to the long stable rose up before them and they crossed the threshold.

Where the harrowing hail followed.

He released her hand and attacked the open door, a giant eight-foot square if it was an inch. A mighty shove and it barely budged.

"It's broken," she said on a breathless gasp, no longer laughing. "Hasn't closed for days."

Had that last strike scared her as it had him?

Over the years, he had experienced plenty of storms. Rolled over the ocean with thunder his only bedmate. Worked on deck even when hail bruised his skin. Escaped the fury when he could, weathered out what he couldn't.

But with this storm, these last few strikes? Every hair on his body stood on end, electrified. Was it apprehension that catapulted him on edge? Or anticipation?

Exactly what did he expect?

To be struck down? Struck dumb?

To find the mate of his life dashing from the elements?

*Balderdash!*

He was miserable, wasn't he? Not excited. Not enthralled. Not thrilled to his marrow.

*Keep telling yourself that, Nate, my man.*

The fabric covering his arse felt both stiff and soggy; his exposed skin both chilled and hot. His heart, nervous. His soul giddy.

He was sickening for sure.

And the hell-sent hail kept attacking.

"H-help me get this shut," his mouth chattered out, as the cold seeped in.

Working together, they heaved and lurched the huge door into its rightful place, covering all but one thin strip along one side.

With a laugh that surprised him into stillness, Lady Olivia picked up his jacket where it had fallen and hooked it on a nail over the open corner. "There!"

The sodden weight of the garment helped keep it in place, swaying with the wind but blocking a good portion of the rain and hail. The ice thunked louder now on the low roof, as though protesting being shut out. Good marble-sized chunks flew in through the open crack below the fabric.

She bent and gathered several before flinging them back outside. "Now what to do about this…"

More bemused than baffled, he watched the wretchedly wet lady—hair ribbon missing, braid coming undone; dress sodden and clinging—lift a wheel-less wheelbarrow up onto its nose until it blocked most of the space beneath his jacket.

"Takes care of that." She beamed at him in the murky light. Scents of hay and horse, of mucked manure, surrounded them, but all he could smell was the pleasing fragrances coming off her skin and teasing his nostrils.

He couldn't help but grin back. "Thoroughly satisfied with yourself, are you?"

"Aye, I am. And you too." When her gaze faltered away from his and focused lower, skittishly this time, upon his chest and stomach, he felt the pitch and roll of a deck beneath his feet. Upending his expectations —his life?—all over again.

He unglued his tongue from the roof of his mouth. "Glad am I to hear it." Ran his gaze over the long stable and took stock of their surroundings— before he risked proposing something wicked. Something wonderful.

The former bustling stable was still and quiet now, a dearth of activity, empty stalls on either side of the middle walkway, open rectangles cut out on most, giving light but also granting rain with every audible gust. Beyond that, the interior was quiet save for their out-of-breath pants and the hoof shuffling of only one or two beasts.

That and the steady storm pummeling the old roof. Would it hold? When he'd rode in, he'd seen a mingle-mangle of clay tiles and wooden shingles, from various repairs made over the years.

"Place 'pears deserted compared to this morning." Earlier, it'd been a jumble, crowded with mounts of the men come for interviews, a couple carriages left in the courtyard beyond.

Blinking to fully adjust his vision to the dim interior, he sought out their companions. At the far end, two horses stood in opposite stalls. A monstrous roan and the sweet nag that had carried him without complaint.

Mistress Bluebell nickered a greeting. Or was it Blueberry? He'd only met her yesterday morn when he'd dropped off his daughters at his sister's and picked up the mare, Susanna's husband out of town with their curricle and younger, more spirited equine pair.

His sincere offer to take the stage had met with her resistance: 'twas lovely countryside, she claimed, time he started to get to know it, to decide where he hoped to settle with his girls now that he'd given up his life at sea, etc., etc. He acquiesced easily enough; stuffed inside a crowded stage, or even perched on top the rushing conveyance, was no way to travel, not when he craved open spaces and needed time to contemplate his apology. Contemplate his entire life, more like.

Another snort from Blue-Something drew his attention.

"Is that one yours?" his wit-snapping companion asked.

"For the day, she is. Hey, Sweet Blue," he called through the gloom, comforted that the horse didn't sound frightened, perhaps just a wee bit lonely, "not afraid of storms, are you, girl?"

He evaluated the big brute across from his borrowed ride, the brown mare decent enough but certainly not a goer like the other equine.

Nate might know aft and port better than after-dinner port, starboard and rigging better than society's rigid rules of etiquette, but even he knew a prime piece of horseflesh when he saw it. "And that magnificent beast is yours?"

"Mine?!" She seemed startled by the notion. "I assume it belongs to the candidate before you, a Mr. Tanner."

But if she'd decided to no longer marry, to not choose a mate through the outlandish advertisement, then what was Tanner's means of transport still doing here?

*What was Tanner still doing here?*

*What does it matter, man? You are who she's with right now!*

When a close clash of thunder caused her to flinch, he abandoned the puzzling thoughts.

She tried to hide her discomfort by jerking her gaze from his body and casually casting about, looking beyond him and into the dark corners of the elongated building. "'Tis no surprise—the empty stalls," she explained. "We have no more horses to speak of. Only the one stable boy, Jacob, and at times Jacks, to look after visiting ones."

She spoke so plainly, so matter-of-factly, without any real regret lacing her tone. Only a pragmatic acceptance that saddened him. Few usable windows. Leaking roof. And not a single horse, despite room for a dozen? What manner of disappointments had she faced to be so benumbed to this one? Just how many sorrows had life dealt her?

He forced himself not to inquire.

*It's not as though I have the ready to meet her requirements, to see her happy.*

Regret talking?

*Does she seem to hunger after money to you? Happiness comes from more than plentiful pound notes.*

His own personal philosopher?

Rather than growl at his bisected brain to be quiet, he was prompted to say—minus the chattering teeth, for her hot gaze had warmed his insides almost too well—"I ask you, how can I be so miserably wet in this moment yet so very content?"

*Is it the company?*

*Of course, you debating dunderhead.*

"'Tis odd, isn't it?" She toyed with the loose, wet ends of her disheveled braid. "I had been thinking 'twas a futile way to seek a life's mate—this whole interview and reference campaign. Now I am not so certain I don't think it's *splendid*."

He chuckled. "Faith did seem rather enamored with that particular word, did she not?"

"Awfully so."

"Likely it was on one of Susanna's recent vocabulary lists. Soon to be replaced with something equally—"

"Splendid?"

Another private, personal moment shared betwixt them. Another second for him to long, for one absurd, dream-filled moment, that he was someone else. Someone full of blunt. Someone drowning in riches instead of uncertainty.

She released her hair, gave a hearty sigh and gripped two handfuls of her long, soaked skirts to flop them away from her legs. A few crumbles from the bottom edge of the muddy morass plunked to the ground; most stuck tight. "I have half a mind to scoot the door aside and hang these skirts outside. Let the rain rinse off the wretched mud before it cakes completely."

"I wish you wouldn't," he replied in all seriousness.

"Why ever not?" She drew one finger up her skirt —straight through the thickest, darkest portion of mud—and raised it between them. "You have an affinity for dirt icing?"

If he could lick it from her skin, he very well might. "Because then I would have to follow your example and poke my arse out. Very unseemly."

She giggled.

"I'd really rather not," he said, trying not to laugh as well.

"Be-because," she giggled harder, "then your... hinterlands would get *really* wet?" His *hinterlands* twitched uncomfortably in their mud-caked prison of super-tight superfine. "Nay, the reason I cannot go hauling arse out the hanging door is because then I would lose all manner of dignity." *And I have little enough of that remaining today.*

"Oh, that's rich!" Her face flushed tomato bright with her increasing mirth. "You stand there, no shirt, no jacket, *no hat*"—as if that were the gravest of his sins—"in ill-fitting, thoroughly dirty trousers and you wor-worry about your dignity?"

What was it about her that encouraged him to act like he had as a lad—joking and smiling, with nary a care in the world? Maintaining a straight face only by the sheerest of wills, he managed, "Aye. And how do you know my trousers fit abominably?"

At that she trilled laughter—much like a rabid jackal might—and turned to stroll down the central aisle, toward where his horse and the other were engaged in quiet nickers and restless shifting.

"It might have something to do with..." Casually, she tossed the words over one shoulder, avoiding his gaze—though it sounded as though she battled more joviality—at his expense. "The seam split down the center."

"*Split—?*" His fingers quickly went to the offending area and sludged through the slush until encountering the two-inch-wide gap.

Trailing after Her Joyousness, he muttered, "And now my humiliation is complete. Have you a dry cloth in here? One with which to erase my embarrass-ment?" He held up both muddied hands. "Or at least to wipe my fingers clean?"

Still laughing gaily—and to his utter delight—she corrected him. "Nay, 'tis not humiliation. For you have nothing to be shamed of, sir. Your...um, drawers looked—compared to the rest of you—tidy and nearly white. That is, unless you forwent them this day—and that was pale skin I glimpsed?"

"'Twas me drawers, woman." He advanced with mock gruffness, hiding his own joy, as he approached her full figure, the nicely shaped rear view clear now that her wet dress molded with indecent fervor to those ample, tempting curves. "Washed and pressed and fresh from my satchel this morn.

"So, what am I to make of your earlier offer?" Once he reached her, he couldn't resist the allure to touch. He gripped her upper arm and swung her to face him. "To mend my shirt? Does that extend to my trousers as well?"

Before she could blush, respond, or whip out needle and thread, he saw what he'd done and released her at once, the flirtatious tone dropping from his voice. "Damn me again. I beg your pardon."

"For requesting mending?"

Frustrated with himself, he gestured to the dark smudges. "For dirtying your sleeve."

"'Tis nothing we cannot fix in a trice," she mollified after a quick glance. "Might as well hang my arm outside along with your arse."

A beat passed.

Silence underlined by the softening storm.

Then he gave a crack of laughter, sheer amazement brimming forth. "You, my lady, are a jewel. Are you quite certain you have changed your mind?"

"About...?"

"Marrying." Or not. "Needing all that money." Those "vast sums" she'd stipulated in her advertisement. *Ones I regretfully do not possess.*

"Oh, ah... I really should—" She started swiftly, then fell silent. He watched an odd struggle flit across her face, as though a battle waged—the sparkling joy she'd exhibited with him versus deep-down remorse for some unknown sorrows.

A resolute nod of her head accompanied by a subdued smile. "Quite. Quite sure. But thank you for the flattering thought."

Regret shot through him. Which was patently absurd. Especially as he stood there, dirty fingers, bruised pride and mortified backside—and *not* interested in another go at marriage himself.

But still...

"My sincere pleasure." *And my sincere disappointment. Damn it all to Hades and back, why could I not own that trillion pounds in truth?*

"And mine, to direct you to the pump." She pointed to the back wall of a nearby stall, one sans door. "I'd forgotten all about it as I haven't been in here much, but look—" Coming up from the floor he spied a pump handle. "Someone dug a well inside a stable? That's something one doesn't see every day."

"We think it's the other way around—the structure came after the well. There's another, newer well closer to the kitchen. Mayhap this one ran dry at one point?

"But see here..." She indicated a small puddle beneath a drying bucket. "It appears to be working now. That or the stable's flooding, and fortunately I don't think that's the case."

He surveyed the scene and had to agree. "Well then, one clean sleeve and dress hem coming up."

He marched toward the handle and arranged the bucket directly beneath the spigot. Placed one knee on the ground, he propped his opposite foot flat on the dirt. The position strained every confining seam, but they held.

*Good old mud's doing a fine job keeping me decent.*

*Except for that gap where she saw your unmentionables.* When "unmentionables" came out in a near falsetto, his own conscience mocking him, Nate almost groaned.

*Stow it!*

Beneath the mud-caked fabric, a slight crinkle from his back pocket reminded him of the one letter he'd forgotten to mention earlier.

His lips quirked in a private smile. But then he got down to business. "Come, my lady." With one hand on the pump, he gestured for her to join him with the other. "Let's see your dress as sparkling as we can make it."

Once she reached him, he leaned over for leverage and—

*Rrrrriiiip!*

# 8

## TO BANTER AND TO BARTER

THE IMMEDIATE FREEING across his hindquarters froze Nate in place; the indignity froze his thoughts.

Unmoving, he experienced the ease and give of valued flesh rejoicing at the end of imprisonment— even if the only guard had been a well-tucked seam.

Mortification blew across his cheeks as cool air caressed his—well, his *other* cheeks.

"By blazes, that did not just happen," he said to the sound of her renewed chuckles, the feel of his own rising chagrin. "It didn't."

If he insisted, if he said it enough, perhaps he could make it so. So he brought forth the bucket, put one hand on the pump and gave it a good push. It barely moved.

"Stubborn, eh?" He spoke to the old metal, which was easier than facing the lass as he feared his trousers were about to go the way of his shirt and jacket. Already the cold air breezed past his buttocks and toward his ballocks, threatening to freeze him into a Scion of Shame.

*Good thing you will not be seeing her again. Right?*

Try as he might, Nate couldn't lie to himself.

*No. Not good at all.*

Ignoring his growing discomfort in the groin-and-Gus region, he braced both hands on the pump mechanism and directed his words to the soggy slippers peeking beneath her dress. "If you want the mud rinsed, my lady, bring thy filthy self over."

Sodden skirts swished closer, bringing the scents of rose blossoms and lemon cookies. Scents he wanted to taste.

Without a word, she lifted the weighty fabric toward the spigot, trailing the hem over the waiting bucket.

He paused, evaluating the expectant air between them. Heavy with humidity, with his humiliation, with her laughter...

And his longing.

He couldn't remember a better day. Such an uplifting of his soul. Couldn't remember a time in his life when doing something so mundane—running from a storm, battling mud puddles and miserable clothes—proved so exhilarating. He hadn't thought of returning to the sea in over an hour.

That thought alone staggered him.

One of his hands slid from its grip to brush away the drying edges of the mess centered over her knees.

Only a fraction of it flicked earthward; the rest clung to the once cheery yellow. Now greyed and ugly.

"Your dress," he muttered into the growing quiet as the rain pattered softer and thunder rumbled farther. "The bright sunshine color... It's ruined."

His fingers clamped tight around the handful of fabric and mud squished cold and goopy past his knuckles.

"Doubtful." Her voice was hushed. She shifted closer with a little *Oh* and clamped a steadying hand upon his shoulder, causing lightning of another sort to flash down his arm. "Mayhap fit for cleaning duty and little else, though."

What manner of lady indulged in cleaning duty?

Before he could inquire, the answer came to him. *One not flush enough in the pockets to hire sufficient servants. She's in desperate need for funds or have you forgot?*

Disturbed by how quickly he'd come to care about her woes, at how vital she seemed to his every breath—at how his innards sparked at every subtle twitch and flex of her fingers just inches from his neck—he returned both hands to the pump and pushed down with a vengeance.

An angry squeak and water gushed forth. The cascade splashed the mud splotch on her dress, then splattered up at him. "By the—" He bit off the curse. "That's miserably cold."

She gave a light yelp and started working at the spot with both hands. "I do wish you were jesting, but I will likely have icicles for knees after this."

His shoulder aching at the loss of her touch, Nate pumped again. "Thought ladies didn't mention their legs, or some such drivel."

"'Tis enough!" She jumped back. "Look, the bulk of it's washed out."

Nate thought not but wasn't up for arguing over it. "Here." He pushed hard again before letting go to cup his palms beneath the spray. Rising, he brought both to her upper arm and splashed water over the smudges. "This might help undo the damage."

When she whispered, "I wish you wouldn't," his heart nearly stopped.

His scrubbing motions upon her arm did, turned caressive instead, as he stilled and caught her solemn gaze. "Stop? Why?"

She looked down at his hand stationed over the smeared prints of his muddy fingers. "'Twas your mark. A souvenir"—the words whispered between them—"of today. So I know it really happened." She glanced back up. "So I wouldn't convince myself I imagined it."

His thumb smoothed over the fabric, mud and lemon yellow combined in a stupid mixture that somehow enraptured. "Are things really so very bad, then? That you have to imagine them gone?"

"Nay." Her voice whispered softer. "Today has been that very magical."

Her eyes glistened. Tears? A trick of the murky light?

"'Tis your turn now." Swiping her sleeve across her face, she twisted away and dropped to the pump, both hands primed on the handle—her knees back in the dirt, getting muddy all over again. "I shall rinse your... Your..."

Out of patience with them both, he reached for her and drew her to her feet in front of him. "Why do you keep doing that? Pulling away as soon as I get close?"

She closed her eyes against his appeal. "It matters not. You will be gone before the day is out atop... Atop..." She wrenched from his grip and escaped toward the horses. "What is your mount's name?"

Contemplating his next move, Nate let her go. "Bluebell. Blueberry? Maybe Blue Cheese. Hell, I don't remember."

"You don't remember?"

"Did I not say? She's not my horse." He followed at a careful pace—deliberately trying not to scare her into further retreat. Definitely trying to rein in his rampaging urges. When he reached the edge of a vacant stall filled with hoof-pressed hay and little else, he paused. "I could leave now. Judging from the sound, the rain's lessened."

"No! Please do not." From her place in the center aisle, flanked by empty stalls on either side, she spun to face him, her long skirts trailing in the dirt and returning more mud to the hem. "Not yet. Whose horse is she?"

So, she didn't want him leaving? Wanted to talk about horses? He could do that—for now.

"My brother-in-law's. According to Susanna, the one the least apt to give me grief. Though I have sailed upon many a ship, I have not ridden all that many mounts."

"Nor have I." She started walking again, her destination seemingly the two lone horses stabled near the far end.

So, flirt but don't finalize? Hold but don't kiss?

Laugh, make memories but don't cross that invisible line.

Just where was her line? *She certainly doesn't shy away from looking at me as though she wouldn't mind getting a handful. Could never get enough, in fact.*

He had so many questions about her! A renewed gust of wind slapped rain into the wall and roof at once. Circled around to blow hard against the barricaded door as though to say *I'm not done yet.*

Well, by damn, neither was he.

The musty scents of hay and damp horseflesh were more comforting than a man used to salty sea breezes would have imagined.

"Come now," he encouraged, approaching her with ease so as not to reveal how vital her response—her every response—now seemed. "Have you not more introductory questions to pose? Sixty-three if I'm not mistaken."

"Come now," she taunted over her shoulder as she reached the stall with his borrowed horse who hoofed forward to greet her. "Sorry, sweetheart," she practically cooed to the horse, "no sugar today. I think we may be out." Then to him, all trace of cooing gone, "I thought we agreed to do away with that nonsense."

"Not a bit. For I find nonsense with you surpasses ordinary with others."

She fixed her gaze on the gentle mare and stroked fingers down Blue-Something's muzzle. "Prettily spoken, Mr. Nathaniel Oliver, but after your entertaining revelations of earlier, what else can you give me in return? Something worthwhile?"

What could he give her?

Answers? Kisses? Unsure of her response to either, he chose the one thing he thought she might find tantalizing enough to barter for: "I do have one other letter. One I haven't mentioned before."

That brought her around again, to the symphony of rumbles rattling the earth. Along with another wince she couldn't hide. "Oh? Another mistress letter?"

Was she afraid of storms? Or simply startled?

"Not until you work for it." Three slow strides brought him to her side.

She gripped the topmost worn-smooth timber and arched a fine blond brow at him. "And just why would I want to see that?" she asked as though he'd offered her a peek at his beetle collection. "To *read* that?"

"I think we'll both gain another laugh from it, likely a hearty one. Now, not another word until you earn it."

"Written by another daughter?"

He remained mute, lips pressed firmly together.

She stared at him, considering.

*Please, please, my lady, play the game just a little longer. Let me earn that elusive kiss.*

His nose reveled in her nearness, the fresh scents she imparted over and above that of dusky, stale stable.

"All right, then. Let me see…" She still clutched the rail with both hands, but he sensed a softening in her posture, a lessening of her guard. "Are your parents still alive? Do they live with you? The heavens. Do you enjoy stargazing? I wager the sky above the ocean goes on forever. What was your most exciting day aboard ship? What about the most harrowing?"

She counted off the first five questions by tapping different fingers against the wood, and continued to do so as she began again, becoming more resolute with each one until she'd tapped off all ten, then started anew. "Uranus. Discovered 1787. How long do you think it might be before another planet is sighted? What would you name it if you found it? Are you a church-going man? What is something you look forward to every day? Have you any profound regrets that stay with you? Any staggering joys?"

A sigh that lifted her shoulders and expanded her lungs followed—he knew because he couldn't help but follow the sway of her heaving bosom—then she turned to him, leaving one hand on the rail and gesturing with the other. "There now. Eleven, I believe. What does that earn me?"

*Half my heart on a platter, the other half soon to follow.*

Shaking off the fanciful thought, he slowly pried his fingers into a pocket, probed the dampened fabric, and came out with a slightly drier, only partially saturated letter.

"From Susanna," he said a mite sheepishly, handing it to Lady Olivia and watching her break the seal with care as he spoke. "She sent me off with this one yesterday morn. 'In case you come to your senses and pursue the lady in truth, I want you well armed,' was how she put it."

Pausing as she unfolded the creases, she caught his gaze. "What does it say?"

"Haven't a clue. To confess, I was so surprised by her words that I didn't think to ask." When she started to flip open the last fold, Nate thrust his hand over the page. "Wait." He curled his fingers around hers. "What of you? Any profound regrets? Staggering joys?"

Something in the words themselves, in the way she'd voiced them, had reached deeper than anything else today. Touched a buried, lonely part of his soul. One that yearned to break free. Made him hunger to ask her a hundred—nay a thousand—questions and to listen intently as she answered each and every one.

"Yea to the first; nay to the second." Not giving him time to ponder her abrupt response, her avoidance of a real reply, she slipped her hand from his loose grip and began to read aloud.

"*'To the Lady Seeking a Spouse: You will do no better than Nathaniel Oliver, a kind man with a caring heart and a generous spirit. He's—'*"

"Read much more," Nate muttered, already regretting the impulse to share Susanna's misbegotten letter, "and you will put me to the blush."

"Hush now," Olivia admonished before continuing. *"He's not miserly of purse nor sour of temper.'"*

"Regular damned paragon, I am."

At that, she glanced up from the page. "'Twould you button your lip till the end, you just might be."

"Aye, aye, ma'am," he said with only a wee bit of sarcasm. Rubbing a hand beset by nerves across his chest, displacing any remaining moisture with a few swipes across the hair-dusted plane, he invited, "Pray, continue."

"'As to his intimate nature—'"

"Good God, how did she sign it?" He grabbed for the sheet.

"Nuh-uh, Mr. Impatience." She whipped it from reach and turned her back to him, holding the page through the railing.

Pray God Blue-Something ate it.

But no, the mare was snoozing, standing on the far side, having lost all interest in visitors not proffering treats. *Traitor.*

The blame woman laughed and fluttered the page, taunting him. "Oh, this is grand. Definitely worth eleven questions." She *tsked* her tongue. "I cannot wait to hear what your sister writes of your 'intimate nature'. 'Tis likely to put *me* to the blush."

He heard a growly noise emerge from the vicinity of his throat.

"To continue... 'As to his intimate nature, I am

convinced his affable and considerate disposition will only convey, leaving any woman he truly cares for counting the seconds between kisses, longing for the moment his lips, his body, once again possess hers.' Well."

As Nate near strangled on the stiflingly thick air spanning the space between them, the blighted sheet fluttered to the ground.

Got clomped on by a hoof. *Poor timing, Blue Ruin.*

"Gracious. There is more, but..." Her voice took on a breathy, beckoning quality. "Mayhap that suffices."

"Well, hell. That was the most cork-brained idea she ever had—writing it, that is. And I had—inviting you to read it. *Lips counting the seconds till his possess yours?* What a bunch of clap-trap."

"Oh, I do not know..." It took a full three seconds before the lady circled to face him, wearing an unreadable expression. "Just *once*..." she said, "if only for one memorable time, I would adore being possessed by a man's mouth."

*By yours. By your mouth.*

Did she speak that last part? Or did he hear it because he wanted to?

"You would, eh?" he spoke roughly, his words a harsh scrape against nerves gone raw.

Her gaze affixed to his lips, and a thousand buzzing bees swarmed his insides. She jerked her head in a single, decisive nod.

To the devil with waiting. *With wondering.*

Nate stepped forward and clasped her shoulders. "Possession it shall be, then."

9

# A BLAZINGLY BOLD OFFER

HER NEARLY IMPERCEPTIBLE NOD, her gentle easing forward into him got completely undermined.

Overridden.

Blasted to smithereens.

By the tremendous spike of lightning that slammed into the roof. Deafening them both. Rabble tumbled downward. Horses whinnied and reared. Olivia jumped into his arms and let out a yelp that barely penetrated the ringing in his ears.

Nate's stomach took a tumble. Feet braced. While his mouth cursed. What else was going to stop him from claiming her?

A simple, bedamned kiss. That was all he was after.

It wasn't as though he was trying to bed the lady in a barn!

*Oh no?*

His "That was some strike" was lost in the thunderous echo booming around them. His brain got lost somewhere between his navel and his thighs.

She felt so wonderful against him. So right. As though he'd held her a hundred times and lived for naught but the next hundred more.

A waft drifted past his nose. Something ephemeral, and not nearly as pleasant as the fresh scents emanating from the warm bundle in his arms.

A niggle of concern told him he should recognize the foreign smell. He ignored it, pulled her more securely into his embrace.

No longer could he hear the raging rain or a horse's shuffle... Only the throbbing of his heartbeat racing through his ears.

Her delicate fingers clutched at his chest, then curved around his waist and back. "Goodness." Her lips stroked his skin. "That was right overhead."

Tremors shook her entire frame.

So stout and sturdy. *Healthy* against him. He tightened his hold. "Tell me true. Are you afraid of storms?"

"Not particularly," she answered just as loudly, both of them all but yelling to be heard over the stunning roar in their heads. "Why do you ask?"

"You jump every time there's a close strike."

"No, I jump every time *you* come close. I am twenty-seven years old. Do you have any inkling of the number of men I have been this near who weren't a relative?"

Before he could respond, she took a step back.

"Do not cry craven on me now," he told her, his tone deepening without intent. "For I want to be touched, Lady Olivia, and by you."

"I am not—"

He eliminated the distance between them and gripped her upper arms, desire displacing the acrid scent trying to compete with her alluring one. "You *are*. You are braver than you think." His words both praised and dared. "Go ahead. Be bold."

The waft came again. Too light to be identified, but wrong somehow. He sniffed. What the deuce?

*Be mine*, he wanted to shout his longing to the churning heavens above. *Be mine*, he needed to beg the charming lass before him.

Be. Mine.

But then his pulse started to calm. The clamorous ringing became a hum. And the crackle of flame licked past his ears.

He looked up, releasing her. A telltale orange glow shimmered beyond the weakened ceiling.

*BE BOLD*, he challenged.

*Be mine.*

Why did her daft ears have to go and tempt her with that last part? Wishful hearing, mayhap. Still cracked from the blast, of a certainty.

So strong and protective he was, making her weak in the knees every time they touched. A resourceful, practical sort, she wasn't used to having anyone take care of her. Having his arms around her was the stuff of long-discarded dreams. And, thanks to him, her unintended deception continued...

Her heart nearly soared. Why was she so relieved every time he inadvertently stopped her from confessing all?

*Because you do not want to taint this magical moment with anything that might—will—ruin it.*

And bring everything to a crashing halt.

Only once had she been so free with another, so very intimate.

*Once.* With Jim. The boy she'd been sweet on, who was equally sweet on her. And the last time they'd touched? She was but fifteen, soon to add another aching year to her top, but fifteen! Twelve aching years since a man had touched her. Or her him.

*So proceed forth. Be bold, with him. Or do you want to wait another twelve years for another chance that may—or may not—ever come to be?*

"Smoke!" His guttural cry pierced the veil obscuring her eardrums.

She glanced upward and the memory of another destructive fire fanned to life. "Oh no, not again!"

"Not *again*?" But she need not answer for he was already scaling rails and climbing upward. "The pump!" he yelled from his precarious perch near the smoking beam, ducking as flames started to lick in through the jagged blast.

The sight took her back to the razing of Amherst, Juliet's favorite property, after careless care of a candle set the place to blazing. The unending hours of night, with all who were able, racing betwixt well and flames, arms protesting the weight, lungs straining with smoke.

Trip after sweaty trip, lurching through the eerily black, orange-lit hours until dawn, heaving buckets of water as fast as they could upon the ever-growing flames until the sun brought the truth: the home a growing, glowing skeletal mansion now, doomed to be ash and fodder for the wind.

Not savable, nor salvageable.

Certainly not inhabitable.

Most everyone's belongings gone up in smoke...

*Just as your dreams?*

Blazes be damned, nay! She would fight this fire as though it was *her* stable, on *her* property, not allow Juliet—*or yourself?*—to suffer another loss.

She whirled toward the spigot, grasping for the bucket.

"See what you can do there, while I—"

Renewed thumps *pinged* and *plunked* against the roof overriding his words.

More hail. Lovely.

*No time for sarcasm, Wiv.* She scrambled back to the stall and wasted not a second swinging one leg over the pump handle, placing both hands on top and straining downward till clear water splashed forth into the bucket. Again. And ag—

"Don't get it too full! Too hard to lift." Renewed pattering from overhead accompanied his shout. "It's pouring again. Bring what you have!"

Carry-dragging the bucket, she met him halfway.

"Good girl." He took the burden and ascended again, getting splattered where the roof had given way. Slanted missiles of rain and hail pounded his skin.

The muscles in his arms and back strained gloriously when he heaved the bucket upward, sending the watery cascade to the base of the flickering flames.

The flames. They snagged her gaze. She watched them crawl inward, threatening the structure... *Please, no.*

"Olivia! Another!" The bucket dropped and she pushed past the heavy swish of skirts and memories to bring him what he needed.

"Here." Watched helplessly from below as he strained toward the growing flames, attempting to douse them before anymore flickered inside.

"The horses!" she yelled as one of them stomped. "Should I take—"

"Nay." The bucket soared three inches in front of her nose and hit the ground with a clunk. "Another!"

Forcing the pump to cooperate, she glanced up.

His booted foot slipped on the rail and fear seized her throat. "Take care!" she squeezed out past the constriction. *Dear funny, wildly attractive Nathaniel, do please take care.*

Time blurred. Arms stung. Water splashed. Tears threatened.

Back and forth, over and over, until she functioned automatically. Pump, heave and drag, lift, lift, strain-lift. *Splash. Plunk.*

"Move!" The second she scooted aside, he dropped straight down and went for a refill. "Have you any other ideas? Another bucket?"

"I'll look. For blankets too." Why hadn't she thought of that sooner? Maybe she could beat the flames back. She scanned every inch of the interior.

Searching for anything they could use to douse the flames, she ran up and down the center aisle. Behind her, he made another trip to the pump. Above her, the heavens cried. Great, angry sobs that shook the earth and sent infinite tears pouring down.

"Finally!" A lone saddle blanket slung over a lower rail. She ripped it free and rushed back. "Found one. Someone must have left it behind this...morn..."

Once again he stole her breath. Utterly.

Oh, not because he'd sent her on an errand. Not from the exhilarating thrill of waging war against the elements. Not because she'd just run the length of the stable and had never been much of a runner...

But because he stood halfway up the wall, balanced with one foot on the railing, the other on the feed bin, ducking down so he could look at her, while sheets of grey slanted in and slashed his face and shoulders, stomach and chest heaving with his breaths.

Especially because of his smile. Generous and light and so devastating that she stumbled to a halt, the blanket clutched between her hands, soggy fire-flies flittering around and lighting up the usually sedate area around her heart. "Nathaniel?" His name escaped on a haggard whisper.

"It's out." He indicated the singed, smoldering hole in the roof. "Our efforts helped, but Mother Nature did the bulk."

He straightened his legs till first his head and then his shoulders disappeared past the tattered, washed-out, smoke-wisped remains of roof. "You should see this, Olivia. Feels ripping!"

Most certainly, it looked ripping. Strong, empowered man, overcoming adversity. Muscles bulging from effort, shining from sweat and excitement—and rivulets of rain.

Raw lust rammed into her so hard she staggered.

She wanted to climb up his brawny, sculpted body and join him.

Well, why not?

Intending to do just that, she headed forward. But a barrage of white flashes brought his head in. A swift leap brought his feet back to the ground just as hers faltered.

"Whew!" he exclaimed, approaching. "'Tis not over yet."

He'd barely gotten the words out before one of the loudest cracks of thunder yet battered her ears. During the auditory assault, he stared at her, eyes alight with his own inner fire, body glistening *everywhere*.

Rain and sweat slicking skin and making her mouth salivate. Gracious. He tempted more than warm berry tarts fresh from the oven on a cold winter's eve.

His black trousers hung low on his hips and she gripped the blanket so hard, her fingers cramped.

"Goodness, Mr. Oliver," she said to cover her nerves and the quick shake of her arm she employed, hoping to loosen the sore muscles. "I thought I told you to hang your duff outside, not the rest of you."

That twinging palm took itself straight to his water-beaded shoulder. Covered muscle and swept outward once. Drops went flying as he remained motionless, save for his deep breaths. Her palm swept twice more, starting higher at his neck, and the beads danced along his chest and upper arm. Then her hand glued itself above one strong, flexing pectoral and stayed there, trembling (just like the rest of her).

And miracle or mayhem, simply touching his warm muscles soothed hers, took the sting right out of her numb fingers. Sent awareness harking lower... deeper...until intimate lady parts cramped too. Lonely and longing.

"Nathaniel," escaped on a sigh. *Brazen liberties, Wivy.*

He didn't so much as flinch. Just grew harder, hotter beneath her touch. Didn't so much as hint at a smile or quirk an eyebrow. "Never was any good..." How was it everything in her vibrated to his deep pitch? "Any good at following directions."

Her fingertips pressed down, met sinew over bone, were teased by the light smattering of fine hair covering places not scarred. "Somehow I doubt that, Mr. Oliver. Your superior would have thrown you overboard."

The firm muscle beneath her hand jumped. "Or in the brig."

"Aye, that." This close, his earthy scent banished the singed tang that tried to invade the air between them. "Or made you walk the plank."

"Did I not invite you to call me Nathaniel or Nate? Which you have done several times already…"

"Daringly, I know." Could she help it if in her heart, she already thought of him as *Nate* but she kept trying to force her lips to put distance between them? *Right you are, Wiv. That's why yours are tingling at the nearness of his?* "Although, should I not have been referring to you as *Captain* Oliver? According to Mr. Hastings' notes, that would have been more accurate."

"I wish you would not." He held her gaze as if imparting a confidence. "*Captain* makes me long for the ocean. *Mr. Oliver* only makes me feel older than I am."

"Nathaniel, then." For Nate seemed far too intimate. "And what is wrong with yearning to return to the sea?"

The muscles she'd caressed turned to stone. "That life is behind me. I now have three energetic sprites to look after and raise into refined young ladies. They mean more to me than the ocean. *They have to.*"

She sensed what it cost him to admit that out loud, the struggle between twin desires. Duty over dreams.

Her eyes nearly closed at the pain revealed in his. Stoic resolve overtook it quickly enough, but she'd glimpsed a hint of what must be a great struggle. As she tilted her forehead toward his chest, ready to rest upon his strength, her eyes glanced past her fingers. Shock had her jerking back.

"Oh my lands, what happened here?" A new worry screaming down her throat, she traced the vertical line of splotched pink and purple that ran down the front of his shoulder and disappeared into the crease of his arm. Something she'd not noticed before. "The fire. Did you hurt—"

"Nay, my sister's homemade shirt and jacket of torture, nothing else." She leaned forward and kissed the bruised area.

He gave a sharp inhale. "Don't. I'm all that is sweaty."

She deliberately breathed him in. "No. Musky. Strong. Divine..." The rain had washed him clean of sweat and grime. Left behind the scents of impossible sunshine and hard-working man. So much better than the applicants who came drenched in flakes of snuff, dog dander, and copiously perfumed, as if that would cover bodily odors and a lack of bathing.

"I didn't don the ill-fitting garments until this morning and by then 'twas too late. Had no idea quite how uncomfortable they would soon become."

Another light kiss of her lips to his tortured skin. Another clench of her fingers upon his chest. Another lurch of her heart, knowing how very limited their remaining time. "Seems to me as though Susanna needs sewing lessons—"

"Fitting lessons, more like."

She stroked his glorious chest again, pressed her thighs together refusing to acknowledge the growing ache between them. "Given what I have learned, I'm surprised you arrived wearing anything at all."

He stared hard into her eyes. One breath, then two. Everything in her began to flutter anew. "Olivia, I—"

Mr. Tanner's brute of a beast chose that moment to step back, bumping into their stall. He then swung his hind end against the railing. Loudly. Accompanied by a couple of snort-toot noises, the kind a gentleman *never* made in front of a lady.

What had he been about to say?

When he remained silent, she chuckled to cover her embarrassment, lifting her hand. "Think he's trying to tell us something?"

Nathaniel's came up to capture it, press it right back against his chest. A gentle curve lifted his lips, a soft glimmer sparked in his eyes, but still he didn't laugh, kept his voice low when he answered. "No idea, but he's given *me* an idea. My poor, beleaguered hindquarters feel like they have been encased in a coat of armor since that groundward topple."

"Uncomfortable?"

"Extremely. I now hold mud in great disfavor." Bringing her with him, keeping them tethered—her palm to his chest—he backed up a couple steps until he bumped into the solid planked wall behind him. Then he moved them both to the side, out of the continuing drizzle. "Time to clean it off my posterior, and in a manner much, much more dignified than exposing it to the elements."

With that, he wagged his derrière against the wood with exaggerated motions, sent flakes and chunks of dried mud flying and dropping.

Olivia lost any remaining composure. She started laughing at his playful antics while he somehow managed to maintain a straight face as he sawed his bum across the boards—until he winced. "Agh!"

"Splinter, sir?" She laughed all the more, her brief embarrassment fading. "I could have told you that was a likely outcome, that yours was not the best of notions."

He paused, glanced down at his chest and shifted his hold to her wrist. "I think 'twas one of my finest notions, my lady, especially if it prompts you to clutch me just so."

She followed his gaze to see her nails pressed deep, a single drop of blood where at least one had pierced his skin. "Nate!"

She struggled to free her hand.

He wouldn't have it.

She struggled all the more. "Nate, what are you—"

Eyes closed, his head thumped backward into the plank wall. His hold didn't slacken in the slightest. "Woman," he said with a pained expression, "when you say my name like that, I..."

*You...what?*

Needing to know, she came closer, swung her other hand between them—and saw she still held the blanket in the crook of her arm. "Here." She shoved it against his stomach. "Cover yourself, you knave." She tried for a chastising tone, but failed. "You will put me to the blush else!"

His head righted itself. Eyes opened. But he made no move to release her grip on his flesh. No motion to take the blanket.

"'Again', you said earlier. Has this structure caught fire before?" he asked.

'Twas three full seconds before she could answer. "Not this one." Tongue thick in her mouth, she moistened her lips. "Another of Ju— Of *my* properties burned recently." *Drat me to dawn and back! When am I going to stop lying to this man?*

"The devil you say! My lady, you have the worst damn luck—er, pardon the language." His hold on her fingers changed from imprisoning to caressing. "I fear, once again, that my conversational abilities are sorely lacking after years spent with only rough men for genteel company."

"No pardons needed. You converse just fine to my way of thinking. Besides..." Slowly, carefully, she eased her impudent nail from his flesh, then placed her fingers tenderly over the spot. "Confessing to one's sins, I should think, would mitigate a few of them. Or so one might hope."

*And are you thinking of your sins here? Your lies?*

She opened her mouth to confess all.

"Ew," he exclaimed, wrinkling his nose, and any confessions she was about to utter evaporated. He gave her fingers a pat, released his hold and reached for the blanket. "Wet horse. Is any smell more pungent?" He used it to blot the moisture from his chest and arms, even scrubbed it across his head. "And when one is thunder-soaked, more welcome?"

"Here. Let me." She took charge of the blanket and shoved his shoulder one way while she scooched the other until she could wipe his back—every beautiful, scarred expanse of it. "So what might your *real* mistress have written, I wonder, had we given her a chance?"

"I could let you ask her"—his voice deepened with the sound of true regret, or it could have been him ducking when she tilted his head forward so she could rub his neck—"but that might prove difficult."

"Pray, why? A bit uncomfortable, perhaps? That I can understand. Or is it that you're leery of what all she might share?" Her brisk motions slowed. "An intimate secret or four you don't want bandied about?"

"Not at all. In truth, I'm curious what she might say about me. Intimate secrets abounding or otherwise." He straightened and turned, catching the blanket up between them. "Nay, my lady, the sole reason you may not consult with her is because she does not exist, seeing as how I do not now nor have I ever, had a mistress."

He may have given a casual shrug, but she wanted to twirl around and shout *Hallelujah!*

"As you can see," he added, lifting both arms out to the sides, drawing attention, however unintentionally, to his magnificent musculature and deplorably dressed—as in *un*dressed—body. "I am not exactly a lofty lord mired in mistresses nor excessive money."

"Oh, dear. That does present a problem."

"Oh, dear, indeed. So here I am, under false pretense and could not possibly warrant further consideration—even had I sought it." Was that regret shading his eyes?

She should know. Should recognize regret as no one else.

For years, had it not shaded her heart, her very being?

*So be bold.*

"Instead of bantering about like a rooster with no hen," she told him archly, "you ought to be *persuading me* to compose you an authentic one."

10

A DELUGE OF DESIRE

"AUTHENTIC?" Time pressed in as he tasted the word, evaluating what flavor to give it based on her intended meaning. "You would compose an authentic one...for me?"

The sudden intensity in his eyes told her the moment he decided.

And that look, that wicked glint, shook Olivia to her core.

Nerves gaining the upper hand, she dropped the blanket and whirled around. "Erase that from your hearing!" she ordered, stealing away. "I did not mean—"

Strong hands grasped her upper arms and halted her retreat. "Explain yourself." Warm breath husked over the back of her neck as she stared at the long, dim row of empty stalls. "Tell me exactly what you *do* mean. Compose an authentic...what?"

"Would you make me say it again?" Her question ended with a squeak when he tugged her to him, brought her back against his torso, her bottom cradled by his hips, arms curved solidly beneath her breasts.

"Aye, I most certainly would," he spoke to the shell of her ear and her entire backside melted against him.

She stayed silent, absorbing the new sensations. Had she ever before had the entire length of a man aligned behind her? His muscular frame supporting—

"Olivia?" His arms tightened, as though encouraging true confession, and the words rushed forth.

"A letter. From a former mistress." Then realizing how absurd that was—how could she offer to be a mistress to any man? How could *she* aspire to such a position—in jest or in truth—when she was naught but a virgin? "About how you *kiss*, I mean. A kissing composition. 'Tis all."

He uncoiled one arm and trailed his hand up her side and past her shoulder until his fingers rested lightly upon her nape.

"And what of kissing?" he asked, speaking against her skin, doing that very thing—kissing, she was sure of it—up the side of her neck, sending exquisite tremors through her. "What pile of suds would you land me in should my kisses not be to your liking? Is not an absent letter of reference better than a critical one?"

As though emboldened by his nibbles upon her

neck, she grew determined to taste his lips. To prove to herself his kisses couldn't be as satisfying nor as stimulating as the gently seductive press of his fingertips on her nape, smoothing her damp hair off to one side as though preparing a sensual assault there too. "But of course your kiss would be to my liking."

Was that his tongue traveling the recently exposed skin? *Oh, fiery furnace, now my belly's gone and pitched toward my knees!*

"How can you *know* that?" he asked as the breath behind the words tantalized her tummy to come back and tumble through her middle. "Is not a disappointing kiss worse than no kiss at all?"

The haggard sound to his voice ripped up her insides. Gave her the strength to jerk free and step away.

Would she be forever disappointed? Would the reality destroy any desire for more?

If Lady Juliet's former husband's, Hairy Horace Letheridge, *forced* kisses were anything to measure by, disappointment was the least of her worries.

Revulsion...

Disgust...

Resignation.

She hadn't been afraid (not after that first devastating time) when Lord Letheridge cornered her, not truly. But only because Juliet confided Leth never could consummate their marriage, no matter how he tried or boasted about it.

But for an old fart with a puny poker, he was stronger than expected and his clutching arms preventing escape, his unwelcome mouth assaulting hers... 'Twas the stuff of night terrors.

*Terrors Nate could banish forevermore*, the shameless part of her tempted. *Even if not perfect, not perfectly in line with all of your dreams, would Nathaniel's kiss not be a preferable memory?*

*Aye. If I could just fortify my ranklesome nerves long enough to—*

"Do you hear that?"

All she heard was the furious pounding of her skittish heart. "Hear what?"

"The rain's halted. No lightning nor thunder since the fire went out."

If he was going to start talking about the *weather*, for gracious' sake, then that was her cue to end this charade once and for all, no confession necessary. No dreams dashed—or realized either, drat it.

"Come, Mr. Oliver..." Defying the lead weighing her feet, she stepped aside and indicated his horse. "I shall see you two off so you can be home before nightfall."

"Hardly."

"Did you just snort at me?" she asked in a huff, renewing her effort to make her heavy feet behave and escape before—

He snagged her shoulders, spun her around and tugged her to him. He bent his knees to speak right in her face. "*Mr. Oliver?* What is that nonsense? *Now?*"

Olivia stared.

His beard. What would it feel like upon her skin? Her cheek? Against her lips, or lower still, abrading the fleshy swell of one breast? She unglued her trembling, hungry lips. "I daresay you are *growling* at me."

He growled again. "Had you not repeated your request for a kiss I might believe you truly wanted me gone. But as it stands, I have a kiss or three to give and even more to collect. Afterward, you can compose any damn letter you like."

*Mr. Oliver?* What the devil was she up to?

Had he not suffered up to his eager-for-the-sight-of-her eyeballs? Was *beyond* excited for her...

The flirting had been fun.

The sexual awareness between them more explosive than gunpowder.

The lusty life firing his groin something of a revelation—when had he *ever* ached for any lass with such passion, such urgency?

*You haven't. Not since the first time you—*

*Dash it, don't go pondering the past! I seek to understand Lady Olivia.*

*Give it up, man. She's a woman.*

*I have noticed. So?*

*So therein lies your answer.*

*Indeed.*

Her inexplicable turns from Sexy Siren to Near Nun baffled.

She'd been married, according to the tittle-tattle surrounding her outrageous advertisement. Ergo, she knew about intimate matters between men and women. Why then did she take two steps toward him, then three back?

His hands flexed, keeping her in place. Gazes locked and intense.

For a man who practically had more scars than skin in places, it was a balm to his ego, a comfort to his soul, to see an alluring female staring at him so intently, and with admiration. But then, the quiver of her lip made him pause.

Part of him was roused to anger—was she one of those women who reveled in toying with men like a razor-clawed cat did with a hapless mouse?

The rest of him was just plain *roused.*

Because despite her vacillations twixt hot and cold, seductress and spinster, his instincts told him she wasn't playing him for a fool, but in fact experiencing bouts of excitement and apprehension both.

Mayhap her husband had misused her? Been cruel or injurious?

Mayhap it'd simply been a long time, or she'd married young and never grew into her own.

'Twas past time he claimed her lips—if nothing beyond—and pleased himself mightily in the process.

Before either of them could dither further, Nate brought his hands up from her shoulders to cup both sides of her face. Staring into bright eyes lit with curiosity and eagerness both—and aye, a tad of fear he feared—he walked backward, bringing her with him, cursing when he stumbled over the blanket they'd dropped, but not stopping till the plank wall at his back halted his progress.

Gave him something to lean against, to steady himself.

Holding her gaze, he widened his stance and lowered his left hand, skimming it to her spine and down...down...inching along individual vertebrae until reaching the slight indentation of her waist and then—merciful heaven—fingertips just barely brushing the lavish swell bespeaking her luxurious bottom.

Her eyes flared, swept to his mouth, then back up to capture his hungry gaze. "Nathaniel, I—"

"Don't bother to protest."

"I wasn't."

"Jolly good because this time, I'm damn well not stopping."

"You're not?" She swallowed.

"Not until both of us are satisfied. At least as much as we can be, with our clothes on, st—"

"What clothes? Yours are mostly absent."

He grunted. "Standing in a barn—"

"A stable."

"Soaked. Soggy..."

"Mmm."

"And so damn aroused."

"So very much," she agreed.

He slid his right hand to her nape, threaded his fingers up along her scalp and paused.

Her shallow breaths were as quick and airy as his.

He'd wager the lust-fired electric feeling flying along his skin was matched as well.

As he spread his legs a bit more, digging his boots

in to anchor his balance, he guided her forward until their bodies just touched.

Her full breasts teasing the dusting of hair on his chest; her long skirts billowing forth and disappearing between his legs.

Her exhales becoming his inhales.

Her breath, his life.

Nate dipped his head. The same instant his left hand turned rebellious, slanted another five inches lower and palmed one luscious bounty of arse cheek. He hauled her forward until she was cradled right between his legs—with his cock snug up against her body.

*Jolly good, man!*

Another of those growls she'd accused him of emerged but Nate wasn't paying attention.

Not to anything but the lure of her lips.

Soft, trembling, they met his. Slightly parted and hinting of passion—and shame?

A fine shiver shook her frame. He pulled her impossibly closer, seeking to protect.

Needing to devour.

A slight hum—hers—met his tongue when it touched her lips. He retreated, nibbled the side of her mouth, licked along her bottom lip, groaned when she attempted the same.

His belly wasn't supposed to feel hollow. His knuckles nervous. Strands of hair elated.

He'd done this before. Dozens of times.

*Dozens? Wooing slowly before the swiving commenced? Maybe six, man. Ten at a stretch. You and*

*Ellen weren't much for prologues, going straight for the final chapter—*

To the devil with him and anybody else.

Olivia was in his arms. *Olivia.* Enchanting Olivia.

She was all he wanted to think of. To kiss. To tup.

*Pardon? Don't you mean Lady Olivia? Ease the press of your cock from the woman's stomach, man. You're not about to tup a lady in a barn!*

While Nate damned his crotch and his conscience in equal measure, the rest of his body ignored the struggle, sought to continue its own discoveries.

Lemon, life and longing: the flavors of her lips brushing eagerly upon his own.

Tangy, tempting and totally divine: the shy thrust of her tongue against his.

Sturdy, solid, sublime: the heft and weight of her beautiful frame cradled against his.

He moaned and brought his hands up to angle her head the opposite direction. He had to taste her there too. All of her. Had to stroke his tongue over her jaw, nip along her neck, across her shoulder—

Had to edge back the deep square neckline blocking his path with frantic fingers, ply his ravenous mouth over the full mounds that greeted him.

Her nipples. He had to free them, to—

To—

To listen to her breathy cries of "Nathaniel, please."

To heed her desires—that he hurry? Or halt?

"Nate. I..."

Lips plastered to one side of the fleshy bounty, his hands now gripping her waist, his damn poker trying to poke a hole in the blasted, too-tight trousers as his hips all but sawed back and forth, lewdly forcing his burgeoning length where it hadn't been invited—despite his unrestrained, unrefined attempt at a barnyard bumping.

"Nate!"

He groaned. Took a deep, painful breath through his nose. Held it.

Tried to hold himself still. And listen.

Understand.

Hear what those artless, abandoned gasps really meant. "Mmm, please..." She grazed her nails over his head, across his shoulders, down the bare skin of his back. "Nate, I..."

Her lower half squirmed closer with decadent appeal while her upper half only strained away. Put distance between them. "I think we should—Should..."

*Stop* didn't have to be uttered. Pleaded. Or begged.

*Stop* needn't be whispered, shouted, or screamed.

Because once she leaned back and he glanced down—craving the sight of her, needing to make the most of the pale, silken flesh he'd reddened with his beard...the ruby nipples he'd just begun to uncover...

Once he looked past that salacious, saucy sight, what he saw froze everything. Everything. His harried heartbeat, the blood rushing through his veins, his deplorable attentions.

For his cock head had protruded from the waistband of his blasted, brutally snug trousers.

The one-eyed brute stared at them both with all the impudence of a disobedient child.

*Disobedient cock, you mean?*

"Hell's teeth!" Nate cursed and ripped away from heaven's arms. He spun to the side, faced a row of empty stalls that matched the emptiness tumbling through him.

From delight to despair.

Taking wicked, perverse pleasure in the sexual ache stabbing his groin, settling hard and low in his ballocks, and squeezing up to throttle the very life from his poor, unspent, waistband-strangled poker, he made a fist and pounded the rail an arm's length in front of him. Slapped his opposite hand to his forehead.

"Blast! My lady. Beg your pardon a thousand times. I—" Grit scratched his throat, self-loathing hoarsed his voice. "Forgive me. You are just that—a lady. And—" *Pound* went the fist; *slap-slap* the open hand. "Here I am, treating you like a dockside doxy!"

# 11

## FROM DESIRE TO DISMAY

NOT A LADY. Nor a doxy.

"You treat me like a *woman*," Olivia told him with stark honesty she'd almost forgotten how to admit to herself, "and I love—" *you for it.* "Love it."

"Love being treated like a three-penny whor—?" He bit off the last.

"No, Nathaniel. Stop!" She had to make this right.

The self-loathing in his tone doubled her burdensome guilt. Tripled it! *He* wasn't the one lying since the moment they met.

"How could I?" He cursed himself, rumbled more including "scourge of the seas" and other various epithets she didn't hear clearly when Mr. Tanner's horse chose to loudly break wind again.

"Stinky beast," she muttered, more concerned with the man before her than what the rude equine had for breakfast.

Things between them couldn't end like this—with the innocent man flailing about amid curses and self-directed accusations about lack of control.

Determined to end his unwarranted pain, she stepped forward, plastered her front to his back. Wrapped her arms tight around his waist. Finally—ready to speak as honestly as she dared.

*Now that he cannot see you?*

"Nathaniel. Nate. Stop, please." She commanded his attention now. Every warm muscle in his body tensed to stone. From the rigid set of his shoulders, the sudden tilt to his frame, she imagined he'd gripped the railing with both hands. "Shhhh."

She pressed her lips to his back, only then remembering his torso was nude.

She'd clutched herself around a nearly naked man, and come hail or high water, she had no intention of letting go. Not any time soon. "Please, stop castigating yourself. I promise, you have done *nothing* wrong, nothing I have not asked for—yearned for..."

The humid air, distantly grumbling storm, the quiet, secure stable all shielded them from the outside, created their own private world.

She kissed his back again, the muscles rippling beneath her lips. "I didn't expect this today. Didn't expect *you*. Or how I would respond." Her arms convulsed, clenching him harder, her fingers and palms splaying without conscious volition, attempting to touch more of the slick skin. "Didn't expect to feel so needful, or so wanton at your first kiss. So—"

The pinky on her left hand nudged firm, yet yielding flesh, something definitely not his stomach or abdomen.

*Nooooo.*

"Is that..." She swallowed down the jagged rock that lodged in her throat. "Am I..." Both pinky and ring finger explored the smooth knob of flesh. "Oh, thunder me straight to dawn. Nate?"

He shifted within her hold, manacled her left wrist. Halted further exploration. "Aye, mistress." His voice was gravel. "You have encountered my cock. The damnable tip of it anyway. Told you I was wicked."

Had he? She didn't recall. "Then do not stop me this time."

Gingerly, she lifted her right hand from its anchor on his stomach and brought it to his "damnable tip".

"Oh, Nate." She'd never heard her tone so soft, voice so light. So delicate. "Or should I say 'All hail, Gus'?"

She chuckled. Giggled. Hugged him tighter with her arms.

He groaned. Lurched a thumb's width toward her questing fingers. The rest of him remained rigid, silent.

"Did my ill-timed humor just ruin the moment?" she whispered, uncertain whether to please her naughty side and rejoice at her discovery or let the prim chicken cry craven.

"Ruin it, please," he grated out. "I beg of you. I cannot— Cannot— Oh God, Olivia. *Can you?*"

Fingers trembling—the rest of her quaking—she

altered her tentative explorations and somehow found the courage to thoroughly investigate what she'd barely glimpsed before.

*So it had been him! That most private, most individual part imaginable.* And imagine it she had—what healthy, grown woman wouldn't wonder? And ache? And wish for the day...

To the stifled symphony of Nate's groans, letting the subtleties of his breath, his gasps, guide her, she stroked downward, touching every solid inch of his length through the trousers with her right hand while her left continued to rub the silky top exposed over the fabric.

When had he released her wrist? No matter.

Her arms no longer circled tightly, holding him in place. Nay, he now seemed content, if raggedly so, to stand still on his own, head bowed. Both arms tensed at his sides. *Are his eyes closed?* she wondered. Or was he—

"Are you watching?" she whispered against his shoulder, her question a kiss upon his skin. "Seeing what I do?"

"Aye. Past the shaking muscles of my stomach, where your unschooled fingers are about to take me to task."

"To task? I don't grasp your meaning." But she did grasp how heat flowed off him, threatening to singe her skin everywhere they touched. How his flesh had protruded even farther, his staff become thicker beneath her hand.

She definitely grasped how she'd pushed her

breasts into the solid plane of his back, trying in vain to ease their stinging tips. How her cheek nestled with utter contentment against his skin. How the rapid thumping of his heart met her ear.

Amidst a growl turned into a groan, he clamped one strong hand over hers, arrested the intimate moment. "Lady Olivia, do you not stop ere long, I doubt I shall be able to."

"Your hoarse words sound so very poetic, Nathaniel." Defying his attempt to still her hand, she scrubbed it downward, then back up the thick ridge. Danced her other fingers over the flared, simmering tip, the heat he gave off searing. Memorable.

"What you're about to bring about is far from poetry. Damnit, Liv, if you do not—"

Giving up the luxurious pillow of his back, she turned her head and slicked her tongue over his roughened skin and up toward his scarred shoulder. "Poetry is in the ear of the beholder."

"Wretch." He gave a throaty laugh but eased the resistance trying to block her upward-stroking path. "Wicked wench."

She laughed. "Nay, not wretch nor wench. *Wanton.*" For that is what she'd be the next few minutes: Wonderful Nathaniel's *wanton.*

'Twas easy this way. Safe. She could be naughty without worry.

For why worry? They were clothed. She, at least. His were beyond repair. But they weren't even facing. No chance, even remote, of pregnancy—the reason her young love Jim had given for not culminating their kisses.

No reason why she couldn't indulge, no fear of things reaching a ruinous conclusion. No worry of what Nate might think of her afterward.

For she'd never see him again. Likely, he'd never think of her at all.

And that tiny little thought *did* ruin it. Spoilt all the naughty fun Indulgent Olivia was partaking in. *She'd never see him again? He'd never think of her?*

Almost violently, she gripped his shaft, circled what she could reach. Gave a hearty squeeze and frisked her hand downward, then up. Downward, then—

"Great God Almighty!" Nate wrenched away. Out of reach.

But not before she felt it upon her fingertips—a hot, thick—

"Damn. Damn. Damn!" He swore until he was out of breath. Bent over. Groaned. Cursed again. Wiped his fingers on his trousers' pant leg after shoving *things* back inside.

Slowly, as though she'd done him a grave injustice, he stiffened his spine. Turned. Captured her startled gaze with his blistering one.

The rhythmic drip-drip-*plop* off the roof and into a puddle the only sound save his harsh breath. Even the horses were quiet.

She couldn't stand the heavy silence between them. The accusation in his black eyes. "My, my, Cap'n Nate, but you look like the devil."

"Aye?" His brows were fierce, beard disguising any hint of a smile. Eyes now more thunderous than any of today's weather. "That reached beyond embarrassing."

"What?" Her gaze flew to his crotch. She wished the material gone, the ability to see what she'd stroked.

"Spending like that."

"Like what?"

"A schoolboy. An untried youth. A selfish bast—" He bit off the rest, then finished with a grimace. "Now 'tis your turn."

That brought her eyes back to his face. Sent her stomach spinning back down to her toes.

"Don't step away," he ordered, closing any feeble distance between them, capturing her in his arms. "Do not think for one second I'm going to leave now, with *this* inequality between us."

His hands roved over her breasts but didn't stop there. Firmly caressed her shoulders, her sides. Took themselves right to her hips and pulled her roughly against him. "No protest to make? Nothing to say?"

"Nothing poetic, at any rate." How did she even form that much? "Do I not protest, will you continue to act the ravishing Viking?" *To conquer me?*

Both hands slid around to cup her bottom. He brought her forward until his body stopped the advance. "Complaining, my lady?"

How far might he go? How far might she let him? "Not yet, my sailor."

"Good. Then don't."

And with that, it seemed Nate had exhausted his supply of words.

His mouth crashed down on hers, his lips and tongue a potent force. Seduction, pure and simple is what he did next: Seduced her senses, every one, so that she might sin for a moment or ten and give not a fig for the future, for regrets.

One hand sprawled strongly beneath her bottom, the other hiked up one of her legs and curved it around his body, opening hers in the process. Her knuckles scraped the plank wall when he backed into it again, then her palms quickly found their way to his neck, his head.

The thick, midnight strands of his damp hair slid between her eagerly exploring fingers. The slow glide of his tongue swept inside her mouth and rolled against hers. Tasting, seeking secrets. Swiftly turning her lower half into that dockside doxy he'd referenced earlier.

Why else would she be arching into him, her hips riding his body, pressing her core hungrily, inelegantly along the length of his "spent" staff?

One hand slid down the side of his face, nails scratching through bristle. Crisp, not soft. But tantalizing all the same.

Tearing her mouth from his, she gasped, threw back her head and hung on. For once in her life, she allowed utter abandonment to reign supreme.

Breathless, skirts hiked above her thighs, the only thing separating their flesh, the only single barrier to them being skin-against-skin, was the straining fabric of his trousers.

The beleaguered material slid along her moist flesh as though it were mere butterfly wings.

The long, hard, *hot* press of her sun-drenched, rain-soaked, tender-hearted, sexy-sailor man so close... So very close as he tilted her bottom, angled her open cleft along his thickening lance.

Just not quite deep enough. Hard enough...

She dragged her sensitive flesh over his thick length. Moaned as her pelvis arched. Seeking... Seeking...

She needed him. Not writhing against, but *inside*.

Ins—

A wild, spontaneous cry escaped before Nate latched on to her tongue, enticed it inside his mouth. Where she devoured his taste, his flavor, and forgot how to breathe.

Forgot any semblance of sense or self when he shifted, skimmed one hand from her buttocks to her thigh. Roved his deliberate caress over the passion-drenched skin as he plied his fingers along her cleft.

Their mouths mated, fought, until she lured his tongue to her and sucked hard, mimicking the fury and thrust of her hips. His palm firmed upon her buttock. Fingers danced against her slit.

She strained toward him, lifted and rolled into the forbidden strokes.

She hurt. Ached. Writhed.

Thrived.

Had anything ever felt so tingly? So achy?

Had her lady parts ever clenched so fiercely? In wonder, and in want?

She whimpered, rubbed her breasts against his chest. Warm.

So hot. Slick.

He rubbed her faster down low. Her breasts responded, slid against his chest with the same fervor he'd created.

That's when she realized: her dress—her entire life at this moment—was in utter disarray.

Her bared breasts partaking of their pleasure directly upon his skin.

The wicked strumming he did down low, between her legs... The forceful way he'd taken possession of her mouth. Her very existence since the moment they'd met sent her core circling around his fingers.

Sent her thoughts spinning faster than out-of-control lightning.

Flashes sparked in her loins and behind her eyes. She blinked and pulled back from his kiss, stared at him with a gaze gone hazy, a mind gone numb, a body approaching a scary pinnacle she'd heard of but never—

Never—

*Never*—

"Sinners and saints, Nathaniel!" 'Twas a scream. A whimper.

'Twas a moan. A sigh.

'Twas the most scariest, best, horridly amazing sensation imaginable, as something inside her coiled, tightened...twisted...balanced on the tips of his fingers...hovered there... Then burst into freedom.

Blessed release.

Brief. Too brief. Far too brief—those few seconds that must last her an eternity.

But beautiful.

So wretchedly beautiful.

---

Now, she knew.

At least in part.

Olivia knew what all she'd been missing her entire life. Knew what she would continue to miss, until the day she ceased. Nathaniel. *Nate.*

His warm hands stroking fire along her limbs, his engaging words lifting her cheeks with laughter. His speaking eyes and sincere appreciation bringing life and light—and the seeds of love, drat his muscular hide—into her heart.

And she couldn't keep him.

Not beyond this moment—that had ended.

She gasped, the pain in her chest real now. For she fully comprehended how much she *was* missing, how empty her life.

How barren her existence.

*Damn me to dawn and back, I will never forgive him for this.*

*What about yourself?*

"You must leave. Now." She pushed against his chest, scrambled to unwind her legs from their hold around his waist. Struggled to find her footing. "Saddle your horse and depart. This—" Her trembling hand flailed in the air between them. "This was an error. An epic"—*do you not mean splendid?*—"one. Regrettable," she finished, the truth bitter on her tongue.

The slash of his brows pinched tight. "If what we just shared was a regrettable error, I will eat my hat. My sister's horse. My—"

"Shush!" Her loins vibrated, quaked. Rain began to patter once again upon the roof.

*You will cast him out? In the storm?*

"Go! Just leave, would you? *Now*, dash it! Before the lightning returns. Please!" She was babbling but couldn't seem to stop. Everything she'd ever wanted, ever dreamed, ever thought *never* possible for her was standing a foot or so away and it might as well have been a thousand. A veritable chasm. "I cannot— You do not— Oh, rot me to midnight, just get out of my sight, would you?"

That wasn't a crestfallen expression on his face, quickly erased by stoicism.

It wasn't.

That wasn't a hand he reached out to her before she slapped it away and he reluctantly pulled it back.

Wasn't a resigned nod, an acquiescent bow of his head that had damp clumped-together strands of silky black falling over his forehead, just begging for her to smooth it into place. To soothe the furrows still creasing his brow.

It dashed well wasn't! Because it couldn't be.

Not when their entire relationship was based on lies. Hers!

One of the horses nickered as though in agreement.

*Relationship? Wivy! You castle-spinning ninny! 'Twas a brief meeting, a snippet in time—nothing else.*

Well, no matter now.

For whatever it was, 'twas gone now.

Gone with the turning of his broad back toward his horse— Were those scratches from her nails across the muscular expanse? Dismay rioted her insides, flushed her face until it felt afire.

"Lady Blue," she called out in a shaky voice, both gratified and decimated when he stopped but didn't spin to face her. "If you cannot remember her name, c-call her L-Lady Blue."

Before she could start blubbering in truth, Olivia took the coward's way out—the only way out, to her way of thinking—and ran.

Ran fast and hard, out of the stable and around the side of the manor—with nary a single look over her shoulder at her Departing Dreams as she sensed more than saw Nathaniel drawing on his hail-battered jacket and leading the horse outside to mount. What had become of his shirt?

Nathaniel. How dear to her, he was, and in such an impossibly short time. His daughters and pregnant sister too. How would Susanna get on when her lying-in came? Was this even her first babe—

*Wivy! Stop it! Just run till it hurts. Till he's gone in truth.*

So she did.

Ran through the damning drizzle as though chased by demons. Across the front of the manor, up one narrow side, then wheeling around to cover the same distance again—just in case he had yet to ride off. Ran and ran, ignoring the stitch of pain that caught at her side, dragged her down. Ignored how labored and loud her breathing had become. How her slippered feet stumbled and slid.

At least she wasn't crying anymore.

Ran—

No, now she was gasping, working both lungs and legs harder than she had since—

Thundering thunder, had it only been a paltry hour or two ago when she'd laughed so hard over Augustus the Dangler she thought she'd faint? *No! Don't think about it.*

*Don't think about him. Or laughing. Or longing.*

*Or his kiss. Or all he made you feel. How your loins flourished beneath his touch. How your heart sang beneath his regard. Forget him!*

*Just run.* Oh, but that body! That majestic chest! Those muscles! That smile...

*My breaking heart.*

# 12

# A CHANGE OF DIRECTION (&
DUDS)

MORE THAN SIX soggy miles elapsed before Nate relaxed his guard sufficiently to allow a single thought to cross over into cognizance.

When he did, they flooded in as if he were Noah himself—trying to keep from drowning.

Who would have predicted I'd find her so full of life? So friendly? So very lovely...

*Never have I met a lady so fair. So fun.*

*Or anyone I felt such an instant kinship with.*

*Oh, but Lady Olivia looked so very mournful when she ordered me to go.*

*So reluctant, yet determined.*

The terrain he and his horse now traveled was flatter than where they'd just come.

At least closer to the crumbling manor, a few hills and copses of trees enhanced the view. Intrigued a man to explore. To vision playing a seeking game with his girls. Hearing Hope's giggles giving her away, Faith's quiet admonitions to *hush*. Olivia's flushed-face exertions as they pretended to search in vain...

Her soft moan of repletion that night in their bed...

Lightning flared ahead.

Lady Blue stumbled and Nate's heart hurt all over again.

*God, I'm exhausted.*

And he was, a deep-down weariness that dragged down every dirty, stormed-upon fiber of his body lower than flea spit.

But the immense case of spit-riddled fatigue wasn't enough to stop the onslaught of thoughts now that they'd started.

*What is Olivia doing? Is she thinking of me?*

*Damn, I'm cold.*

*I hope she's warm and dry by now.*

*At least it stopped raining.*

*Is that hunger gnawing my belly? Or huge servings of regret?*

*She sure was pretty. Vibrant. Laughing.*

*Laughing with me over the silliest things...*

*Hell no, that's not emotion pricking my eyelids. It's the wind.*

*Lady Blue is a better goer than I have given her credit for—mile after plodding mile with nary a complaint.*

*Man, my nipples hurt. Stupid-arse body part. Too close to my aching heart?*

Ache it did, even worse than his numb nipples, as scene after scene frolicked in front of his eyes:

Her appreciative astonishment upon first spying him.

Her flattering amazement over his chest. The beefy, nicked-up torso honed by years of labor that he'd never thought much about.

The heart-wrenching sorrow when she took inventory of his scars.

Laughing with her over ripped seams and roasted rabbit. Sharing tidbits about his girls and their antics. Laughing about Gus. Just laughing.

Her lips after he claimed them. Swollen and reddened and wet—

Wet. Would his miserable, muddy arse ever dry?

And now that he sat upon it, why did one cheek plague him as though he had a pesky pebble perched beneath his perch?

A pebble?

No, too tame. It felt as though a stupid bee had left its unwanted stinger plumb in the middle of the right side. Maybe those flushed, bitable lips of hers could kiss it and make the pain go—

*Stop thinking of her! She told you to leave...*

And with clarity and emphasis, if he were honest.

His rebellious mind flickered back to the stables, to the intimate scene he couldn't erase no matter what undisciplined thoughts kept stampeding for dominance.

As he'd held her, reveled in her rubbing against his straining link, he'd clenched teeth and jaw to keep from calling out. To stem a second eruption not planned.

He'd thought her sturdy enough to take him? To slake his lust?

He'd not considered how she'd feel in his arms. How this buxom beauty would fit like exquisite perfection within the circle of his strong, seagoing muscles...

How her flavor, her kiss, the indelible points of her breasts—their heft and bounty—

How she'd fill his heart, his very being... The lonely hours and years he'd made do without.

He hadn't gambled on how she'd splinter within his embrace and from his uncultured touch.

Or how holding her trembling, quivering form in the moments after her whimpered release would beckon, bid him never leave.

But then—

*"Just leave, would you? Now, dash it!"*

The bellowed command threatened to freeze the heat of the memories boiling through his chilly limbs.

*You have said your goodbyes.*

Well, no. Come to muse on it, no, he hadn't.

Neither had she.

Had she?

"Just leave" did not a proper goodbye make. Did it?

It had effectively sent him on his way, that was a certainty.

Well, if not that, then her brokenly cried "Get out of my sight!" had put arse on horse and heels to his exit.

But before that?

Oh blazes, before that...

*"Your chest is the most blessed sight I have seen in ever."*

*"Are you ever going to put on your dratted shirt?"*

*"Applicant twenty-five, what have you done to me?"*

*"I don't think my heart's pounded that ferociously in years."*

*"I think I'm in love."*

*"Might as well hang my arm outside along with your arse."*

*I think I'm in love.*

Her words echoing in his garret—his head absurdly empty and lonely now without the geese flocking to it—Nate considered their remarkable afternoon. The undeniable regret plaguing him now.

Companionship. Laughter. Passion without demure.

He'd found all three today.

Might love follow? And not flippant, laughing love, but real, lasting love?

Had it already begun?

As though to answer, his horse whinnied, lifted her neck in a high, energetic arc.

"Aye, Lady Blue." Nate looked over his shoulder, back the way they'd just come, the sky alternating between light grey now that the roiling storms had moved off after having their say and darker areas hinting at possibly more to come. Then he stared ahead, his cold body swaying with her slow gait, toward their destination. Deep, pewter puffs full of anger and lightning roared. "I'm starting to wonder whether home might lie in the opposite direction as well."

And if it did?

It mattered not. He had a horse to return, a home to seek out and buy, daughters to raise. No room in that plan for love. For Lady Olivia.

*And why in hellfire not?*

Nate kept his gaze—and his horse, with a sharp tug—focused straight ahead. Tried to stop thinking. And failed.

Damn.

Damned cold.

Damnable ache in my chest.

*Damn, man, what you need is a hot bath and a warm wench. I wager you can hire both at the inn tonight.*

The thought of sinking knee deep into clean, heated water should have revived him.

The idea of tupping a pretty barmaid should have brought a lift to his loins.

But...

Nothing.

Nothing but stone-cold, soul-deep misery touched him now. That and a sudden deluge of several more thoughts sure to freeze his insides, if not his poker, right to perdition:

*Goddamn, it's cold.*

*Right buttock still smarts.*

*Who wants an available, willing wench when what I need is a reluctant, unavailable lady?*

More of their exchanges bubbled in his brain,

some of the day's inconsistencies, niggling. Creating a conundrum he really needed to solve.

*Get thyself to the inn,* his cold conscience interrupted. *Get dry and warm, and then decide whether to return in the morning, confront Lady Conundrum, or mayhap, simply spend the coin for a beddable lass—*

Coin?

*The king's own shit! I left my saddlebags and money at her house. Cannot buy a room or a wench, even if I cottoned to the idea. Which I don't.*

His horse clomped to a halt. Snorted a loud breath of complaint out through fluttering lips. Nate squeezed his thighs. "Get a move on, Lady Blue."

Lady *Blue.*

Blue.

*Is Liv as sad as I?*

*I need her.* And he did.

Not just for a laugh. But for life.

He needed to fight for her, at least try for her, even though his pedigree and pockets may be lacking.

*Of course you do, you simpleton! And do you also want to know why you're freezing?*

*Eh?*

*Chest is cold? Nips are numb?*

Eh?

*Lackwit, you still have yet to put on a shirt!*

Nate looked down at the expanse of skin exposed between the sides of the frayed jacket he'd never fastened. "Pin my hide to a wall, proof that she's stolen my wits."

*Dear ma'am,*

*We are splendidly sorry we wasted your time. We just wanted a mother again.*

*But even more, we wanted a splendid wife for Papa so he would stay home this time and not go back to his big boats. So he would smile and laugh and not look off into the heavens with a frown.*

*He is a right fine man and would make you a splendid husband if you change your mind.*

*Your friend,*
*Faith Anne Oliver*


*Dear Mistress Lady Scandal,*

*Papa says I must write a note of apology, but I shall not do so. For in truth I am <u>not</u> sorry, not even a tiny bit. And one should not lie, correct?*

*Since I turned eight (I am now thirteen and a half, going on thirty soon, or so says Aunt Susanna), Mama was tired a lot. Then she was both tired and sick. I miss her since she's been gone. I know she's happier now, in heaven.*

*But Papa isn't.*

*Aunt Susanna tells fun stories of what Papa was like at Faith's age (not that <u>she</u> remembers, being so much younger, but she knows the stories from when Gramma was alive). I used to think <u>all</u> ancient people like Papa and Uncle Drew were sad or grumpy. But Grampa Andrew is even older and he tickles Faith and Hope when we see him. (I am too old for such childish nonsense, you see.) Grampa Andrew does play cards with me (he says I am a great sharp, whatever that means) and he hides silly things for us to find after his visits.*

*Since he left the ocean and came home for good, Papa has played too. It's been wondrous fun. But I think he's very lonely. Either for the sea or for a wife.*

*If you would please marry him, he won't need the sea anymore. We can all be a family. And I won't apologize for trying to make it so.*

*Just meet him, please. His beard is scratchy but I think he would shave it off if you asked. And if you can sew, then I really want you for my new mama. Aunt Susanna takes <u>forever</u> to make anything and by the time she has finished a new dress, I am quite grown out of it...*

THE "APOLOGY" letter from Charity continued in the same vein for another page.

Chilled to the bone, but somehow warmed by the youthful chatter, Olivia sat in the "crypt" formerly occupied by all the boisterous applicants—now eerily silent; simply her and her riotous thoughts as she studied the girls' penmanship and tried to stave off dreams of being Faith and Charity's—and Hope's—mother in truth.

What had she to offer in trade for such honest love?

No money.

No dowry.

Certainly no lands or title.

Only a fraction of the "youth" so prized by wife seekers.

Granted, she boasted a decent education, by feminine standards, but she was no striking beauty.

No great catch.

Only a deceitful—as of today—companion, hiding in a boarded-up room, rifling through a saddlebag she had no right to broach. Reading letters that were never meant for her. Yet treasuring every word, every sentence as though they alone could sustain her past this utterly miserable moment.

How could she have ever anticipated finding such accord with one of Juliet's applicants? Her stomach hurt not only with dismay over how very brazen she behaved, but from the laughter and joy found with Nathaniel Oliver.

Her hands smoothed over the top page as though

to steal comfort from knowing he had placed the folded letter in his saddlebags, had touched the heartfelt, unread words of his oldest two daughters.

She ached, eyes watered and stung at the realization never would she meet the jewels practically within her grasp... Nate's daughters...

*If you were a lady—and not a lying companion.*

Foolishly, she'd stayed outside far longer than made sense.

By the time she'd run herself ragged around the manor's perimeter, finding the drenched remains of his shirt dropped during their mad dash to the stable, she crept back inside, once assured *he* had left and passed the chilly, wind-and-water-dampened time making certain Mr. Tanner's beast was comfortable.

More showers moved in—straight in, thanks to the lightning hole above—and she remained, petting the brute's long nose, bringing him clean water, uncaring when the breeze gusted through the open door, drenching her all over again.

"Penance for my sins?" she asked the big roan, guiding him to the driest stall before lingering all over again, reluctant to face her impending return to Dutiful Companion, *Lady Imposter* being so very thrilling for the afternoon.

A long shiver-inducing while later, she'd snuck past Cook's back—who was scouring the sparse shelves in the pantry, muttering about stingy supplies —intent upon escaping upstairs to her room to dry off and change.

So how was it she instead found herself quivering

in her rain-soaked, passion-drenched dress, staring at the small selection of items Nate—no, from now on, she'd best think of him as Mr. Oliver—had left behind?

*Because you all but ordered him to leave!*

Aye. And have regretted it every second...

⸺⧓⸺

UPON REALIZING that he was exposed to the elements —embarrassing, if helpful, flash of insight, that— Nate reined Blue to a halt. Pondered a few seconds and then turned her around, facing the way they'd just come. He sat upon his shifting mount, evaluating his options. Contemplating which direction seemed *right.*

The "right" one? He craned his head to look over his shoulder toward Duffield, where a slight rise blocked the view.

Or the "wrong" one? Slowly, testing how it made him feel, Nate turned in the direction of the shoddy manor he'd just left.

The stretch he'd just covered all but beckoned.

What to do?

Knowing what he *wanted* to do but undecided on how to convince his rational mind, Nate swung one leg over and jumped to the ground.

"Sorry, girl," he said, loosening the girth so he could steal one of her two blankets. "I'll make it up to you somehow, sweetheart, but for the moment, I need this one more than you do."

The fact that he'd ridden miles wearing nothing but boots, battered jacket and split-asunder trousers only went to show how very discomfited the entire day had made him. No wonder the encounter with the one family he'd passed, going the opposite direction in a landau with the top down, had brought titters from the young lasses, a blush from the missus up front, and a roaring scowl from the man wielding the reins.

As he whipped the blanket free of its creased-in folds, wishing eau de equine was as easily shaken off as a few stray horse hairs and dust motes, the rhythmic plod of hooves and a creak of wheels drew his attention. Two gentlemen in a cart pulled by one not-in-a-hurry horse topped the rise from the direction of Duffield.

The younger man handling the reins wore a cassock or similar long black garment, proclaiming him a man of God. Nate knew he'd never seen the chap before but there was something vaguely familiar about the older passenger sitting next to him, even though a broad-brimmed hat shaded the second-man's face.

As they approached, he heard snippets of their heated exchange: "banns", "outrageous", "what you're asking me to do, Uncle" and so on.

Nate nodded a polite greeting when they neared and guided Blue over to the side of the road, more interested in wrapping the horse-warmed blanket over his weather-chilled skin than in exchanging pleasantries with a pair of strangers, somewhat familiar or not.

Deep in conversation betwixt themselves, they rode on by with a brief tip of their hats.

Nate's focus returned to his horse. He readjusted the saddle and tightened the girth. "Ready to earn your oats, girl?" Nate scratched encouragingly against her dark brown shoulder.

"Shall we let practicality"—*Don't you mean your heart?*—"decide for us? Since I'm out of coin, the only way either of us finds a roof over our heads tonight is to ride for home— Uh, Liv's home. I know I'm asking a lot of you, but you can do it." Even if Olivia declined to see him, it would be close to, if not already, dark by the time they returned.

And no man worth his salt wouldn't retrieve his saddlebags. "We really have no choice." She wouldn't deny him and his horse refuge for the night, would she? "The stable, Blue. I'm confident I can promise that at least."

Nate never knew whether Blue planned to agree or balk because a yelled greeting interrupted his one-sided discourse. "Hail! Captain Oliver, is that you?"

It took a moment for the question to penetrate his befuddled brain. When it did, Nate turned to see the older gentleman standing in the cart, wobbling more like, as it rattled to a stop, hat doffed, a perplexed look upon his lined features.

Recognition was slow in coming.

The man took in Nate's sorry state of dress—er,

*undress.* "Captain Oliver? I say, you have not taken ill, have you?"

It was the tone of voice that finally did it. The caring, sincere manner and friendly countenance the man displayed was memorable even though Nate had only met the solicitor once. "Mr. Hastings?"

"Aye, 'tis me, Captain." Hastings' surprise was evident. "What say you? Why are you traveling this road? Now? And...*alone*?"

Why did the man seem disappointed by that?

"'Tis the way home." Or it was.

Blanket bound, Nate remounted and turned Blue to face the pair.

Still standing, Hastings queried, "But did you not meet Miss H— ahm, the er, ah *lady*?"

"Lady Olivia?" Warmer now, if more because of his decision to return and try again—*Try for what, man? Marriage?!*—than because of the slightly scratchy wool blanket draped across his shoulders, Nate settled in the saddle, barely avoiding a wince from that dratted right cheek. "I did indeed meet the fair lass and found her much to my liking."

"Then why—?"

"I was not seeking a wife," Nate gently reminded the older man. Was he daft? Prone to forgetting? "And 'twas just as well for she also changed her mind."

"Oh? Do tell."

"Said she'd abandoned the whole marriage scheme altogether." *So 'tis up to you to change her mind, is it not?*

*To convince her of what?*

*To at least spend some time with me, by damn. See whether my modest savings and navy prize monies can even begin to make a dent in the fortune she requires.*

"And after all that work?" Hastings looked crestfallen. The color leached from his face as he muttered, "And praying? I was so sure..."

The man's companion gripped his arm when he wavered. "Uncle?"

Nate stood in the stirrups, ready to dismount at a moment's need. "Sir? Are *you* ailing?"

Hastings shook off the megrims and waved Nate back into place. "'Tis only a lack of fishing—er, ah *fish* on my plate, I assure you."

The other man chuckled. "Not eating enough, Uncle?"

Hastings ignored him to ask Nate, "Are you certain you must leave without...without... *Must* you go?"

"Nay. In fact, sir, only just now have I decided to return. To talk some sense into that special woman."

"Capital!" Hastings exchanged a gloating look with the younger man beside him, and, as though assured by Nate's decision, resumed his seat. "See, Nephew, what did I tell you?"

"You told me..." If a man of the cloth could be said to roll his eyes, this one certainly did, and in such a spectacular fashion Nate wondered if he'd perfected the move from the pulpit when interrupted by tardy parishioners. "That God loves fishermen and meddlers," the younger man said in a resigned voice, but with an indulgent smile as well.

"See here." Hastings motioned for Nate to ride abreast of them. "What of the blanket, Captain Oliver? Have an aversion to actually wearing your wardrobe, do you? Enjoying the rain a little too much?"

Nate explained his clothing conundrum, starting with Susanna's ill sizing and ending with torn seams. The suspected splinter, he kept to himself.

"Well, sir," the solicitor assured brightly, "we are delighted to be of assistance, my good man."

After Hastings introduced his nephew, a Duffield-area vicar he'd persuaded to journey with him, he offered Nate the contents of their cart.

"Can't go courting with nary a stitch on, Captain. 'Tisn't decent!"

Courting? Was that his aim?

"Aye," said the younger man, directing his horse and cart away from the middle of the road, "on that we all agree."

He set the brake and jumped down, going to the back where tarps had been secured over several tall stacks. "We have been visiting my flock, you see, the less prosperous families, sharing food and clothing Aunt Margaret gathered from the good folk in the village.

"If my loquacious uncle will let me get a word in, sir, I am sure you can find something to fit. Might not be in fine fashion or it might have a patch or three, but I can guarantee all is clean and you, sir, appear a man in need if I ever saw one."

# 13

# FROM SADDLEBAGS TO STAIRS

-One leather saddlebag, worn but of good quality.
-Two letters, already read and committed to memory.
-The remains of a meal: crumpled handkerchief (embroidered with ~N.A.O.~ in one corner, with blue waves sailing up two sides); oilcloth, folded neatly but exhibiting crumbs and the lingering scents of gravy and roast beef.
-A leather bag containing coins (something Olivia easily identified by the clink and heft of it, not by opening the leather ties and counting).
-A pocket watch.

But no ordinary pocket watch.

Because this, Olivia did open, carefully, when she noticed how the latch caught.

*To my Ollie—*

### Forever Yours, Em
### 1765

Fifty-ish years ago. So his father's, then? And if Nate carried it, was his father deceased? What about Em? Emily, perhaps? His mother? He hadn't mentioned either today...

Was he alone in the world—as she was?

*Aye, you Lying Lady Imposter! He's all alone, surrounded by three adorable daughters and his sister and her family. He's not likely to be pining for you.*

Aye, but he would be wanting this watch back, and his money.

Ignoring the odd shiver that bolted through her, cold of heart and damp of spirit, she found her wet attire appropriate punishment as she replaced every item in the bag, save the watch cradled in her palm. Moving slowly, she rose from her kneeling position next to her bed.

Her bed, where she'd arranged everything beyond the girls' letters for her methodical inspection, after lighting a single candle to see by, her window being one of the boarded ones.

The temporary room she'd claimed while she and Juliet worked through applicants and the rest of their meager stores the last few weeks—that, and battled rain and roof leaks—was actually one of the nicer chambers she'd ever lived in. If, that was, one could discount the lack of easy light and the peeling wallpaper, thanks to the leaks.

Her eyes darted from the saddlebag on her

mattress to the pair of buckets on the floor, both brimming from catching drips all afternoon. This was actually the second bedchamber she'd inhabited, when the first started requiring upwards of *four* buckets to catch four separate drips. She'd given up a working window in exchange for slightly drier accommodations. Which meant the buckets had to be hauled down to the ground floor.

As though beckoned, her gaze drifted back to Nate's prized and precious possessions.

What to do?

*Quit whinging over what's lost, that's what, Wivy.*

*Lost? As though you were the one to find him?*

In fact, was it not the other way around?

Hadn't she found something wonderful within herself, thanks to Nathaniel Oliver?

Had not the sunshine from his kiss shone a light into her dark, lonely soul? Illuminated that which had not been known before?

A lightness, a sureness, a *flirtiness* freed by his very presence?

Even now, as downtrodden as part of her felt at his departure, did she not also feel inherently stronger? Invigorated?

*Why, I do!*

Moving with purpose now, she went to her single traveling trunk, which contained half of everything she possessed. (The other trunk, with books and mementos, the useless trousseau she'd sewn and embroidered as a naive girl—still waiting for Jim's return—resided at another of Juliet's properties, one of several the new widow had promised the right suitor in exchange for his money.) Lifting the latch and lid, she foraged for one of her handkerchiefs.

No initials adorning its corner, but marvel that Juliet was with needle and embroidery, the fine scalloped square did have an accurate rendition of their beloved Henry: In one corner, battered ears, whiskered face fairly grinning with deftly sewn threads, eyes alight with mischief. A tiny brown mouse trapped beneath a front paw.

Smiling, she placed the pocket watch within its pristine center and folded both treasures together before placing it, too, back inside the saddlebag.

After she emptied the buckets, refreshed her body and attire, she would secure his possessions downstairs in the study, and then compose a letter herself. One to Mr. Oliver, by way of Mr. Hastings, explaining and apologizing for her deception, begging his pardon, and returning his belongings.

It might not change the outcome, but at least she'd be taking action.

Exhilarated by the thought, she grabbed up one of the buckets, blew out the candle—after the tragedy at Amherst, no one ever left them burning unattended—and rushed from her room, taking care to descend the first flight of stairs. But once near the landing, the sound of muted voices coming from the room she'd vacated a lifetime ago stalled her steps. Had her turning down the narrow hallway.

Juliet. Oh, ruinous, rainy day!

*I forgot all about her! Grand companion I am.*

Hearing laughter on the other side of the door, she set aside the heavy bucket and paused, watched as a fluffy paw shot out beneath, tufts of sandy-orange fur protruding from between each razor-sharp claw.

Glad for the distraction from her chaotic thoughts, Olivia knelt to rub her index finger across Henry's furry leg.

Her hair flopped forward and a couple beads of water dribbled from the tips. Gracious, shouldn't it be dry by now?

Henry swiped his paw over the droplets, the cat's antics bringing forth a shaky smile. *Good for him. The floor could certainly use a thorough mopping.*

Cringing at the strands uncomfortably glued to her neck she'd been too distracted to notice earlier, she gathered the sodden mass over one shoulder and whispered, "What exactly do you think they're discussing now, hmm?"

*Do not mean* doing?

As quietly as she dared, she tested the doorknob, intent on releasing Henry, but it held. *Locked.*

Heavy, rapid thumps coming from the direction of the stairway heralded a new arrival mere seconds before she heard the corridor-muted shout. "Lady Juliet!"

Giving Henry's paw one last pat, she rose and hastened toward the landing to intercept Jacks. "Shh-hh." She motioned behind her, in the direction she'd come from. "We ought not interrupt them, I'm thinking."

"We 'ave visitors," Jacks began, only to break off and exclaim, "By the devil! Miss 'Ales! Ye... Ye look..."

Drat. She hadn't known it was quite that obvious. Self-consciously, she raised both hands to the hank of hair residing over one breast like a waterlogged washcloth. She started to wring out the mass, then stopped when more moisture rained toward the floor. "I'm a muddle. I know."

"A muddle?" Jacks reared back, appraising her from soaked skull to soggy slippers. After taking in the muddy streaks trimming the bottom of her once-pristine dress, his thoughtful gaze returned to hers. "I'm seein' more than a mere muddle, I could be fergiven fer thinkin'."

Double drat! It was beyond apparent, then? What she'd done with Nate? Er, *Mr. Oliver.* Cavorting with an applicant not hers to begin with? Mortification poured through her veins like syrup. It was one thing to indulge herself as she had. Another to have someone else discern it.

Thank God the only man *witness* to her crime was gone. Gone for good.

That last thought should have brought a semblance of comfort. It didn't.

Down the hallway, Henry swiped his paw like mad from the other side of the door, a stick of orange fur waving furiously at her to come back and play.

"Wot's up with 'im?"

Relieved Jacks' attention was no longer on her bedraggled person, she answered, "I think he wants out."

"That's seen to easy enough."

When the manservant started to move past her, Olivia halted him. "Nay. The door's locked. I tried a moment ago."

"*Locked*, ye say?" His surprise and satisfaction at what that implied mirrored her own. "Well, 'Enry can't be wantin' out too bad or 'e'd be yowlin'. 'E's just having a spot o' fun wi' ye."

"Aye." Blowing a mental kiss Henry's direction, she started down the hallway, away from the door. Dumping her bucket could wait. "And locked"—she indicated Jacks should follow—"is how it shall stay until *they* decide to open it."

"That big Tanner feller?" Hearing Jacks describe anyone as *big* was almost comical. "'E's the one, ye think? The one that'll save Lady Juliet from the lonesomes?"

"Judging by how they reacted to each other? Aye, I sense marriage in her future, this time of her choosing, thank heavens."

Jacks snapped his fingers as if just remembering something. "An' that's why I ran up 'ere to fetch 'er. A vicar's 'ere."

"A vicar? *Here?*"

"Aye. From Duffield. Claims Mr. 'Astings sent 'im over to do a wedding." His explanation spun circles around her mind. Like a flock of geese, mayhap? "I gather 'Astings himself is out in the barn, stabling the 'orse—"

"A wedding? So soon?" Goodness, the solicitor

had certainly been confident; she marveled at how much. "But the banns—"

"That's fer you and 'im to discuss. Me? I'm jus' relayin' the message."

Mr. Hastings was all that was thorough.

Olivia had observed that when she accompanied Juliet on her initial excursions to his office at the onset of this marriage scheme. Mr. Hastings had been the one to suggest obtaining references and medical and financial histories from each applicant. It was also his idea to have each man sign a penalty clause so Juliet's identity wasn't compromised. But in the spirit of *being* compromised, it was Juliet who insisted on requiring a letter from each man's mistress—but only after Olivia stupidly put the notion in her head.

Now, with a bit of after-light, she completely concurred on the benefits to be gained by securing such a reference.

If Mr. Hastings had arranged for a vicar to come here to conduct a wedding, then a wedding they'd likely have.

Yet, given what the low murmurs and soft sighs now coming from the sitting room might be indicating... "We need to stall him. Downstairs."

"Eh? Fer 'ow long?"

As long as they take.

"Until Mr. Tanner and Juliet emerge—whenever *they* choose to," she told Jacks decisively, her own body still feeling the achy effects of abbreviated lovemaking. The warm rush of *any* lovemaking. "No one is to interrupt their, ah...the interview."

"Right-o." She swore Jacks winked at her. "An' 'ow do ye want I should stall the man?"

"I'm not certain." She cast about the spinning geese for ideas. "Invite him to dinner. Serve him a scone."

Reaching the top of the stairs, she halted, recalling her state of dress and the need to exchange her drippy garments for dry ones.

In the several weeks they'd resided here, not once had anyone called upon them (discounting the invited applicants, that is). And now she had a vicar to contend with? *Now* of all times? How she was supposed to compose and conduct herself in front of a holy man after the amorous adventures and sinful lies of the afternoon? It didn't bear thinking upon.

Oh, but certainly the afternoon did...strong arms, warm lips, the taste of first sunshine and then a male chest...

"...an' the semen...yer dress..."

Her wayward thoughts cartwheeled back to those few stolen moments and distracted her from the current one. Surely she could be forgiven, then, for not instantly grasping the sentence that now hung heavily, expectantly, in the air.

"Well?" Jacks prompted. "What 'ave ye to say?"

Fine black hairs, sparsely coating muscles so very hard...their texture teasing her palm... "Hmmm?"

"Aurr-*hmm!*"

Recognizing Jacks' frustration at her inattentiveness, she replayed what he'd just said. Or at least she attempted to.

The semen...your dress.

Wha—?

Vague comprehension was enough.

Olivia blanched. Had to put one forearm against the wall to keep from crumpling in a swoon. What had he said? "Semen?" she squeaked on a whisper. *"On my dress?"*

Whipping her long skirts this way and that with her free hand, to and fro and up and down with hurried, harried motions, she searched frantically for the condemning evidence.

Jacks cleared his throat. Then cleared it a second time when the first failed to gain her attention.

When he coughed so loudly a third time she was almost knocked off her feet, she halted her frenzied search. Reluctantly looked up. Paling all the more under his knowing gaze, she murmured, "Aye? What is it?"

"I *said* that seaman was back too, the navy man, the one from earlier. Come to pay 'is address to ye— I mean to the *lady* of the 'ouse."

"He's here. Now?"

Jacks grinned as if her express purpose was puttering about for his exclusive entertainment. And as though he thought she was doing a bang-up job of it. "Aye, an' askin' to see the lady of the 'ouse. Again."

*Again.* When they both knew *she* was the only female he'd spoken with.

*Oh, lying Saints above. Lord forgive me.*

Realizing it was a bit late to petition His pardon, especially given how one of His minions currently resided downstairs, she released her hold on the wall and started to slump toward the floor. Given how crumbly the rest of the abode, it wasn't too far off to consider she might literally slink right on through...

Too fast for her own good, Jacks grabbed both her shoulders and steadied her, only easing his grip when she nodded her thanks. He rocked back on his heels. "Yes, indeed. When the cart rolled up, hauling all three and pulling his 'orse behind, the gent asked fer an 'audience' with yer ladyship, Lady *Olivia*."

Well.

*Well.*

And wasn't this her afternoon sins coming back to bite her on the arse?

# 14

# TWO… EIGHT…

<hr>

SHE COULDN'T RECEIVE callers dressed like this!

*Nor can you make them wait. They asked for Juliet and 'tis edging toward evening. Do you want them knowing what you suspect occupies your friend and employer?*

"Heavens to hell, what a mess."

After Jacks went down, heart hammering in her chest hard enough to break through, Olivia paused at the landing to compose herself. Out of breath with nerves and anticipation both, she recited, "Three, eleven, seventeen. Three, eleven, seventeen."

*It is just a few moments, Wivy, and then you may escape to your life assisting Juliet and being invisible to everyone else.*

Why wasn't that reassuring?

As outwardly calm as one would strive while practicing their bow to the queen, she descended the stairs, readying herself to greet whatever—*who*ever— lay beyond.

## A Few Minutes Earlier

"Where were you this afternoon?" Nate asked Jacob, the young servant who had helped him unhook the horse from the cart and stable both that gelding as well as his Mistress Blue. "During the storm?"

His gut clenched at how differently the afternoon might have gone had the young man, all gangly limbs and long reddish hair that needed trimmed, been present.

"Fishing, sir. After all you gents got here and most all left. The storm riled up more than I 'spected, so I stayed and waited for it to move off 'fore coming back."

"Catch anything?" Mr. Hastings inquired. The solicitor had watched their equine efforts with a tolerant, if encouraging, expression after sending his nephew on up to the house, to alert the unsuspecting residents of their arrival.

"Nah, not today. Yesterday, though, I caught three," the boy boasted. "Small'uns, but Cook made do."

"Ah." There was a gleam in the old codger's eyes. One Nate recognized—a fellow angler, it seemed.

"Then there was Henrietta to see to," the boy put in, still explaining his absence. "She finally—"

"Henrietta?" Where were his people? The lad, though sturdy enough, wasn't a brawny strapper. The straw-head couldn't have been much more than Charity's age, mayhap younger, judging by the youthful pitch of his voice, the smooth skin of his face.

"Aye." The youth beamed at him. "Come see."

After a brief detour that more than explained his earlier absence, the hand turned back to settling the horses and Hastings indicated to Nate they should step outside. "A fisherman, are you?" Nate asked idly, stepping through the wide walkway the boy and he had made, scraping back the stubborn door.

"Every chance I get. Which is far too seldom." Hastings gazed toward the manor, then shifted his attention back to Nate. "Now that my nephew's inside, we can speak with ease."

"He doesn't know of Lady Scandal? Of your hand in marrying her off? I thought nearly everyone did by now."

"Not nearly to the extent of my full involvement, no. He's only aware of the whole ruffle vaguely. Avoids the town papers and tattlers, you know. Here in the country, pious man of God and all that."

Now that the rain had moved off, a fly buzzed around his face. With practiced ease, Nate reached out, caught it and flicked it away. "So he thinks... what? That he's here to perform a wedding?" During the brief ride back, not only had Nate's mind finally connected several bewilderments of the day, but he'd been privy to the enlightening arguments—er, conversations—between his two companions as well.

"Or a semblance of one, aye," Hastings concurred. The man shifted in place and brought his bent fingers up to rub the bottom of his jaw as he confided with only a small touch of guilt, "He thinks Tanner and Lady Letheridge are reuniting after a long absence. That her father kept them apart—not terribly far from the truth."

"What about myself and Olivia?"

"Olivia," Hastings mused, looking sly once again. "Not *Lady* Olivia?"

"It never would have been 'Lady Olivia', but Lady *Letheridge* had you intended to give me her actual title or name." He'd pieced that together while pondering something Tanner had said while they waited together in that crypt so many hours ago.

Nate looked out toward the garden where everything had started—for him, at least. Overgrown yet still calling to him even now. He blew out a hard breath and returned his gaze to the other man. "I admit, your subterfuge worked at first"—and wonderfully, given how the scant time with her passed in a joyous blur—"but she confided a couple things, *almost* shared a few others, and I was coming to realize your deception, and hers, right about the time we met on the road."

"And yet you returned with us."

"That I did."

"Even knowing she possesses not land nor fortune?"

"Correct."

Hastings measured him with a leveling look, one that would do any commanding officer proud. "Then go claim her."

*I intend to.*

AVOIDING the formal entry he'd been delivered to this morning after stabling his mount, Nate led Hastings through the back—past the garden and into the kitchen entrance he'd used with Olivia. The pair of them followed their ears toward the front of the house to find the burly footman and Hastings' nephew jawing at the bottom of the stairs.

A strangled whimper, one reminiscent of the first sound he'd heard her make a lifetime ago, drew his eyes upward to see her descending the stairs slowly, regally, fingers trailing along the peeling wallpaper. Her attention flittering everywhere but upon him.

To his hungry gaze, hers was a magnificent, compelling sight.

Soft blond hair undone from the braid, in an untidy coil over one shoulder, dress drying but mud stained and wrinkled. Lips swollen—from his kisses? Yet even now, her teeth had sunk into the bottom one.

*Should be* my *teeth.*

Cheeks bright from the pink hue that covered her face and the exposed skin of her neck, that flushed the pale, barest hint of the generous swells of those magnificent breasts his tongue had laved that afternoon. Starved to taste again.

She looked both weary and wicked, tired and totally glorious to him. And she wouldn't meet his eyes.

A curious dip to his stomach firmed his resolve.

*I am not leaving without you.*

<hr>

WHEN OLIVIA finally braved acknowledging each of their visitors, she wasn't prepared for the indulgent smile of the usually stern Mr. Hastings. Wasn't anticipating the resigned sigh of acquiescence from the vicar he introduced whose name she missed.

Certainly wasn't prepared for the casually attired country farmer who'd come to call along with them, sweeping in and then stepping to the front door, still ajar from whoever entered last, and putting his shoulder to it, heaving it back into position. A broad-brimmed straw hat shielded his face, loose-fitting blue chambray shirt his torso.

Though she already knew his identity, it was still a breath-stealing shock when the country gentleman stood tall after shoving the cumbersome door back into its place. Nate? How had her Nathaniel Oliver from this morning, sun-bronzed bare skin, muscles galore and smiling eyes been replaced by the narrowed-eyed stranger? Determination glinting from beneath the hat he swept off to make his bow, revealing a crease around his damp hair. "Lady Olivia."

"Nay," she corrected immediately, staring at a spot over his shoulder. No more trickery. "Olivia only, no lady. No title."

When she chanced a half-second glance, he gave a single nod, that resolute gleam in his unreadable gaze not changing, but chilling her even more than the uncomfortable cling of her dress.

How was it that seeing him again was both a boon and the greatest pain in memory? Her fingers clenched, the tips of her nails gouging into her palms as she fought the urge to reach for him, to brush his dark hair back from his forehead, to check the bruising that had likely grown worse beneath his arm. To touch the crisp hairs of his beard. To taste his lips once again.

*To finish what you began in the stable?*

Aye, that. How she wished for that, fervently. But now, a man of the cloth stood before her. Mr. Hastings as well. "Gentlemen, welcome." She cleared her throat and loosened her fists. Immediately, though, she clasped her fingers together in front of her waist to stop their trembling. "I, ah, wasn't expecting visitors."

An understatement of epic proportions.

Her heavy, inappropriately dirty dress became an unbearable weight. Why had she not ordered them gone instead of greeting them with closed arms? "Forgive me for receiving you so hastily."

Mr. Hastings' eyes crinkled in a smile, softer than

what she'd seen from the efficient solicitor before, despite their several meetings. "Dear Miss Hales, dare I hope all our efforts yielded fruit? Lady Letheridge? How are she and Mr. Tanner getting along? Captain Oliver and I saw his horse still here. May I assume that bodes well?"

She couldn't keep her traitorous gaze from straying to his. *Nathaniel's*. A shudder shook her frame at his steely glimmer. She jerked her attention back to Mr. Hastings.

"I believe so, yes. They are, ah..." She thought back to the murmurs, the slight squeal she'd heard only minutes ago. "Right in the thick of things I believe, the *interview*, that is." She bit her lips against explaining further and then blurted out, "One I choose not to interrupt. I will retrieve them, but not until later. Would you gentlemen care for..." What could she offer? Weak tea? Weaker spirits? "A beverage? A-a scone?" sputtered from her the longer Nate stood so near, his presence reaching out to her though he did not.

"A scone?" the vicar repeated with a pinch of his brow.

Right. Scones were for tea. Not a full meal. And it was definitely past dinner, closer to dark than not.

"Nay!" Jacks all but barked. "No scones. Not..." He fell silent once all eyes turned to him. He eyed Olivia, then stepped over to whisper, "Had one earlier. Not fit for company," before he moved back to his stance near the stairway.

Had they run afoul of Cook again? Oh dear. The

long-suffering, woefully paid woman had threatened to make meals fit for grubs and naught else if Juliet didn't liven the pantry. Olivia sniffed. No scents reached her nose, nothing but damp horse and the impossibly sunny scent coming off the man who had taken two steps closer in the last moments, and now stood but an arm's reach away.

"Or mayhap dinner?" Egad, her voice rose on the last syllable. Was she offering things that did not exist? "You gentlemen have traveled a distance today and must be famished."

Pork and pig bellies, what was she going to do? Given all the calamitous times of late, Juliet had not been entertaining, *nothing* and no one beyond the interviews.

They weren't prepared for guests!

"We are not here for food." Nate finally spoke, and the welcome timbre sparked along her spine.

"Of course not. You—" Her flittering gaze lit upon the vicar and Mr. Hastings as her thoughts spiraled. Words from earlier spun dizzily through her mind... *Seaman. Semen. Wedding.* She gripped her hands tighter, to prevent her palms from slapping her cheeks. "Jacks said something about a wed*ding*?" And there her voice went, going all high again. Her head jerked back to Nate. "But why are *you* here?"

"For—"

"Oh!" she shrilled, the pitching of her stomach too much to bear. To be this close and not touch? Not embrace and inhale? 'Twas surely suffering being visited upon her, for her sins. And not the ones of the flesh. The ones of deceit. "You are no doubt here for your things."

"Nay, I—"

"I will retrieve everything. Return posthaste. Remain!" She aimed her palms at him like weapons. "Remain here—" With a whirl of body and a swish of skirts, she swirled to the staircase, rounded Jacks and raced upward.

Heart pounding.

Feet racing. Eyes tearing.

A creak. The second tread.

A moan of despair—hers.

Goodbye.

'Twas coming again. Nate was here, but soon to say *goodbye*. Again.

How was it that it hurt more the second time?

Slippers soared.

Oh, if only she were a bird, she could fly out the window.

One tear fell. She dashed it away.

Powered on.

Another creak—the eighth tread.

Thumping hearts, what was she going to do?

How was she going to watch him ride off again?

Without learning his most harrowing day serving king and country? Without hearing more about his precious girls?

And then a *crash*. Her right foot sinking painfully deep, through splintered, cracked wood to the sound of her anguished whimper.

15

## ACQUAINTANCES? BAH. TRY INTIMATES

"Olivia!" The cry tore from Nate's throat before she finished her choked-off scream. He shoved Jacks aside and bounded up the stairs, taking them three at a time. Heedless in his race to reach her.

Her thoroughly ruined gown—mud, rain, the trials of the day—billowed on the treads as she half stood, half knelt near the top, her body at an unnatural angle and the bunched fabric keeping him from seeing more.

Behind him, murmurs of concern: "Bandages. Cloths. Clean water. Soap..."

He let the words fade as he focused on the female with closed eyes and head bowed, biting both her lips, fists clenched, one at her side, one near her mouth.

He reached her and grasped her quivering upper

arms seeking to steady and to comfort. "Olivia. Is anything broken? Can you tell?"

A sharp shake of her head indicated not. Moisture gathered on her compressed lashes.

"I'm going to lift your skirt and petticoat, see what kind of damage we might be looking at."

Her eyes should have flown open at that—the liberties! Her mouth should have unsealed to rail and castigate, for no one looked at a lady's bare limbs—no one!

That she stayed still and *silent* and un-protesting, said more than an entire sermon. She was hurting; he needed to know how much.

Gathering the fabric in one hand, he lifted it out, like a shield between her body and the others below. She had one slippered foot securely, if awkwardly, balanced on the solid tread below. But the other? Her foot had gone clean through, most of her injured leg up to the knee obscured by the splintered board surrounding it.

He wrenched his gaze from the top of the pale stocking, and even paler thigh above, and inspected the damage. "How bad is the pain? Did you sprain anything?"

She still hadn't answered him. The hand not holding her dress like a curtain grazed down snagged stockings, started pulling at the fractured edges of the board.

Several scrapes, reddened and beginning to surface-bleed, a few splinters it looked like to him, but he had yet to see her foot and ankle. He wrenched the board aside, surprisingly easy given how feeble the rotten wood, dove his hand inside to skim the rest of her leg and foot. Thank goodness. No liquid heat met his questing fingertips, so no pooled blood. No protruding bone either.

He angled to better inspect what he'd revealed. Along one side of her calf, a deeper scratch, one bleeding more than the others. One that brought a slight moan from her chest when he probed the area surrounding it. He fisted the hand that had been touching her leg and released her skirts with the other. Standing, he cupped her shoulders. "I see a couple of small splinters and one larger that needs tended." She failed to respond. 'Twas as if he hadn't spoke. "Liv. Look at me."

She didn't. Just swayed there, eyelashes swimming, one tear tracking down her face aside her nose, now biting the knuckle of one fist. He gave her a light shake. "Olivia. If you do not look at me now, and tell me what else you are feeling, we are climbing on my nag—make that Tanner's sturdy brute—and galloping for whatever physician Hastings recommends."

She finally opened her glistening eyes at *galloping*.

Finally opened her trembling mouth at *physician*.

"I may have wrenched my ankle." The words were but a wisp. "Nothing broken. What am I feeling? Feel*ing*?" At the last, her voice rang as high as a bell. "How can one describe the Pinnacle of Mortification? *Here she comes, and in the gown of humility: mark her behavior.*"

All right. If she could attempt quoting obscure Shakespeare, then she wasn't gravely injured. So he responded in kind. "*So flies the reckless shepherdess from the wolf.*"

That at least brought a small smile. "And that would make you the wolf?"

Did she realize she had started to quiver all over? The aftermath, most likely, of his arrival twisted up with her accident. "I would be *your* wolf."

And he needed to see his shepherdess warm, her injuries tended, and find out why the devil she fled from him as though he were a demon chaser.

So as the others hovered, he took care to see that she balanced with her hands upon his shoulder and back, and freed her foot. Then he swept her into his arms before she put any weight on it at all.

"I'm too heavy! Put—"

"You are not." He debated for a moment. Took several cautious steps toward the others, using the wall at his back for additional support and checking each tread before placing full weight upon it.

"Miss Hales! You gave us quite a fright."

"How is she?"

"Are ye aright? Miss 'Ales?"

He ignored the voices clamoring around as he neared the ground floor and paused to ask her, "Is there water upstairs, clean cloths?"

"Wa*ter*?" That bell rang again. "You ask that after the downpour of the day?"

"In a bowl, a basin? To clean your leg."

"The kitchens! You should take me there." If her

expression could have conveyed their bodies, they would have shuffled there in an instant.

"And have an audience overhear our pending discussion? I think not." He glanced upward, considering.

"You cannot be alone with me in my chamber." How easily she read his thoughts.

He resumed walking, carefully reaching the bottom of the stairs. Where he halted and spared a glance toward their gawking audience. "I suppose not," he murmured, for her ears only. "I may have been away from society and its rigid protocols for a while, but even *I* know it isn't the thing." But she had *run* from him rather than listen to a single word. Had hied away with the intent of shoving his things in his face and sending him off once again.

Silly widgeon. Did she think she would be rid of him a second time so easily? "Never is it done..." he mused, almost to himself. "To be alone with a woman who isn't a relation. To be alone in her *bedchamber*."

"No, it isn't."

"'Twill likely ruin you completely."

"Relieved you realize— Wait!" With a decisive nod toward their curious audience, he spun on his heel, aiming back the way he'd just come. and began climbing the stairs. "*What are you doing?*"

He grinned. "That should be obvious. I'm ruining you."

She loosed a squeak of dismay. "What are you saying? That you *want* my reputation in tatters? I know I tricked you, but—"

Behind them, a throat cleared—loud enough to summon the dead. Loud enough to pause his feet.

He glanced toward the waiting trio. Didn't say a word, just waited.

"Ah…" Mr. Hastings fumbled about for something in his jacket and held it out. "This one came in late." A letter, a folded one, addressed to *LADY SCANDAL*, in bold capital letters, with the instructions inked below:

*Should things be looking grim:*
*Give to the lady in question if all else should fail.*

Nate read the curious directive after Hastings placed it upon Olivia's middle when she refused to take it, frowning at the folded and stamped letter as though expecting it to sprout fangs and snap at her fingers.

"'Tis one more reference I would bid you to put to the best possible use." Hastings gave them both a nod and backed away.

Had Susanna sent one more plea on his behalf? But nay… For he did not recognize the handwriting. But someone supported his suit. Nate grinned. "Thank you, sir."

He angled back toward the staircase.

"Halt, if you will."

The vicar. Of course.

At the first tread Nate turned slowly. Waited for

the man to speak further. Gone was the affable vicar from the cart, the one who had encouraged Nate to rummage clothing meant for parishioners. In his place stood a man possessing only a few more years than Nate, one with even, unremarkable features and thick brown hair in want of a brush that reminded him of Lady Blue's tail. The countenance and form that on the journey here had seemed unassuming and nonthreatening took on a completely different mien as the holy man confronted what he perceived as an injustice. "I thought you and Miss Hales were already well acquainted, not—"

"Acquaintances of long standing," Nathaniel answered with great confidence, convincing confidence, which was absurd when one considered that their acquaintance barely totaled half a day.

*Yet seemed a lifetime.*

Or at least the beginnings of one.

"*Loooong* standing," he repeated, jostling the female in his arms when she would have contradicted him. "*Intimates,* if you will. Such that there remains some misunderstandings we need privacy to correct. Your uncle will vouch for me, already has, I believe."

With that, Nate let Hastings console his still-vocal nephew while he strode directly up to Jacks, who had worn a scowl since Olivia's staircase mishap.

Would the servant tender a protest? Try to pound Nate into the ground as he had applicant twenty-three so very long ago? No man wanted to admit another would best him in a fight, but Nate had no illusions who would ultimately win should the two of them seek to battle in earnest. The beefy Jacks possessed hands like hams, at least eighty pounds and several inches on Nate's already impressive size.

"Are there others?" Nate asked, instead of seeking permission or giving the other man opportunity to object. "Bad steps?"

As though battling with himself, Jacks' scowl deepened. "I will let you take 'er. Tend to 'er. But if any 'arm—"

"I traveled here this morning to make my apologies and leave," Nate said with a quiet strength, his words directed solely toward Jacks and not something for the other men to overhear. "What I found was unexpected and is more precious than the promised bounty your Lady Scandal offered." Nate couldn't stop his hand from rubbing against the bounty in his arms. "No harm will come to Miss Hales, this I vow."

With a quick glance toward her, noting the mutinous look now adorning her features—also noting her silence—Jacks nodded once and gestured up the stairs. "She's already split through the top one. Avoid the second an' the eighth."

COULD COMPANIONS EVEN BE RUINED? Or was it ruint?

"*Oh, bother it!* Are you really going to let him carry me off?" Her mouth may have implored the men below, but her heart was in danger of soaring.

Nay, it wasn't, she sternly told herself. Her heart was in danger, period. From the man with the muscles and grimly determined jaw.

"Do not complain to them." His voice lowered, lips came so close to her ear that her stomach threatened to drop through the broken tread. "Else you *want* me to give you something to complain about..."

"Nath— Mr. Oliver! You wouldn't!"

He sliced her a look that said he surely would, ascending the remaining treads with a rapid pace that left her swallowing any further complaints.

When he gained the first landing, he paused and glanced down the corridor. "Bedrooms? Upstairs or here?"

Her traitorous eyes gave her away, glancing upward, and he promptly started ascending the second staircase.

"You cannot haul me about the entire way. Set me down. I can walk." She wiggled, unused to being carried—ever. "I'm not the sort of female one gallants about like—"

He hefted her in his arms, ceasing the protest. "Not what sort?"

"You know what *sort* I mean." She waved the hand not clamped around his neck and shoulder. "A delicate flower to be lifted and twirled and toted about like—"

A derisive *pffft* huffed past his lips. "If you think I want a 'delicate flower', Olivia, you don't know me at all."

Her nails dug into his shirt at the back of his neck. "But I don't, do I?"

"Hell, woman, yes, you do!" Upward he went, strong, sure steps taking her toward her doom.

*Do not be so dour. I wager, with him, ruination will be a delight.*

"You know me," he continued. "You know the *vital* parts; just as I know what is paramount about you. You, my dear Liv, *belong* with me."

When had her nails released their hold, her fingers straightened, caressed? When had her other hand—the one tired from agitated waving—aligned itself along her side, to lightly settle upon the masculine hand crooked beneath her knees?

"As to your 'sort'?" he said. "I find it rather exquisite. Not too heavy, not too light, just outright perfect."

"But—"

"But nothing. I could hold you all day."

To her consternation—and utter amazement—she realized he spoke the truth, wasn't overly winded upon reaching the second landing. Wasn't—

"Your chamber?" he demanded so imperiously, she pointed before thinking better of it.

"Nate?" A faint squeak; an even fainter protest.

"O-liv-i-a." A slow, sure rumble of possession.

*Oh, my.*

The swiftness with which he advanced toward the privacy of her chambers and her impending doom— *nay, delight*—had her gasping, "Nathaniel."

His breath hitched, pace stuttered. Then he resumed walking, striding really, and with a vengeance. "You are going to say that again," he told her, keeping his eyes straight ahead, his manner stiff, "just like that once we're alone and I am inside you."

*Inside me?* Flames licked to life everywhere.

"Which one?"

Her stunned brain obeyed the note of command and her arm shot out to indicate the room she'd claimed. But he didn't move, instead stood there, turned his head to stare at her. His slate eyes so close. So *heated.*

"What?" Her voice held a breathy quality she wasn't used to hearing. "What are you going to do?" Or not do? Why had he stopped? "Did you come to your senses? Ch-change your mind?" *About me? Us?*

If so, why wasn't relief swarming through her?

*Because, you silly twit, you want to believe everything he said. That you* do *belong together. That marriage isn't the most buffle-headed notion ever.*

*It isn't! Not between us. We...fit!*

*Then why do you keep arguing?*

*Because I'm scared. He... This... Us...*

"Did I change my mind?" The harsh growl asked the question as though *she* was the buffle-head.

Her door stood ajar. He balanced on one foot—one foot, mind!—and nudged it wider, swinging the door open on creaky hinges.

Then he strode through as though he belonged.

# INTIMACIES ABOUND

How DID her room look to him? Smell to him? Musty with age compounded by the humidity of the last hours... "Forgive the lack of light or air," she apologized, mortified afresh.

"The window tax, I know."

The meager daylight filtering through the cracks in the weathered boards revealed the large space, sparse of furnishings, rug frayed along the near edge, her trunk along one wall. His saddlebag upon her bed.

Also embarrassingly visible were the single full bucket and the dark patch on the rug where she'd yet to replace the other.

She squirmed, the sting in her leg naught compared to the ache in her heart. "Let me down and I can scrounge the candle."

"Not yet, for this suits my plans."

"Your plans?"

He kicked the door shut behind him, a squeaky groan that ended in a solid *thwump*. His nostrils flared, inhalations coming fast.

"See?" she cried, both triumphant and disappointed. "Exactly what I expected. Carrying me is too much for you. You're all out of breath."

"Nay." He turned suddenly icy eyes to hers, and after tensing his hold for a long second, he slowly, ever so slowly, eased his grip and allowed her body to slide, along the front of his.

An action that had her gulping and reveling all at once, when certain things (hard, firm parts of him— one in particular—crossed her flesh).

"Nay," he repeated, cupping her face once her feet gingerly touched the floor. "Not from exertion. From holding back." His thumbs feathered over her trembling lips. "From not being able to do this since you ordered me from the stables."

"Th-this?" Her voice shook more than the great hall chandelier last week, seconds before it crashed to the floor.

"Touch you." His lips followed his thumbs, brushing over her mouth. "Taste you."

His tongue slid inside, and if not for her clutch upon his shirt, she would have swooned, hit the floor as hard as that chandelier. As it was, her tongue stroked against his with eager abandon. He drank from her, giving hint of his own turmoil, and only releasing her lips to murmur, "After I left, I realized I forgot some things of vast importance."

"You mean the letters from your daughters?" Truly, he had snaffled her wits. "Oh. Your *saddlebags*. Of course." Disappointment warred with delight. *Would he kiss you like that if all he sought were saddlebags?*

"Those, aye, but most importantly: *answers*. Of which I will grant you some now and some later and even more after we're married."

*What?* "What!"

"*Married*, I said, and quite clearly I believe. Sounds splendid, does it not?"

"But you do not *want* to marry. You said it yourself—you came to apologize and leave."

"Can a man sound of mind and desirous of your body not alter his plans? I now find the state of marriage looms with all the appeal of treats on Christmas morning. But only if that marriage is to you."

"Oh, but...but—" She stammered around, seeking inspiration. How could she permit things to proceed with him, no matter how she might long to, not when everything was built on a thumper of a lie? *Hers.*

"Your watch!" She made a poor effort to escape his embrace, thinking to lunge for the bed—to thrust his possessions at him before he tempted her with air castles he truly didn't mean. Only to be caught, right back up in his arms as he growled at her. Growled!

"The watch? *Pfft.* Olivia." Her name rumbled from the depths of his determination. "Surely you realize by now? I am only here for one thing: for *you*."

·  ·  ·

AFTER OLIVIA'S uninspired attempt to evade him—evade what welled thicker than that stuck barn door between them—Nate hefted her by the waist and crowded her against the nearest wall. Refusing to release her gaze, brimming with growing ardency and anxiety both, he let her drift downward from his arms, keeping a firm grip on her hips when she would have hobbled off.

"Though we were both initially under some misapprehensions, I assure you, 'twas all by design." Her back to the wall, he leaned in, caging her with his presence. "For you see, Hastings told me explicitly I was being sent to meet Olivia Hales. I am the one who attached 'Lady' to your name. Who made assumptions."

"But I am not rich or titled—"

"Nor I." Despite her draggled state, her confusion over his return, consternation at his fumbled explanations and cumberment over her recent injury, he couldn't help but simply breathe her in. The whiff of sunshine and citrus that even now clung to her skin naught but an invitation. Just begging him to taste anew. To lick all night. "Although my pockets are moderate, they are sufficient. I can keep you in ribbons and lemons *if* I avoid gambling over whist with my oldest."

"You jest, but... You came here for *her*: Lady Scandal."

"I came here for *you*."

"But I— She— You…"

He heaved a hard breath. "Do you not tire of protesting?"

She sighed. "I do."

He traced his tongue down her cheek. "Then hush a bit, hmm?"

His lips rubbed over the damp trail and then he angled his head, seeking her precious seaport eyes in the gloom. "I have some answers to tend before another minute elapses."

"You have *answers*? Nay!" She clapped trembling hands to both sides of his face, nearly covering his ears. But he watched her lips, heard every heartfelt avowal with both hearing and heart. "I have *apologies*. Your pardon to beg.

"In truth, I owe you a bigger apology than Napoleon owes England," she continued, her panicked speech fervent. "And France. And—"

"Ho! Hold right there, Liv. An apology, I'll allow you to tender, but only a wee one."

"Wee? Are you *daft*? 'Twas deceit I practiced, and with you, a professed advocate of *truth*."

"Liv! Stop." He was choking on his mirth. "You dare not make *me* out to be a paragon. For there were two of us in that barn today, being swept along by a firestorm of our own making ere that strike ever hit your lady's barn."

"Stable."

"You would dare quibble over that? Naming the structure where so…*deuced…much*…happened?"

"Aye." She faced him boldly, with shoulders back,

eyes agleam, as though exchanging words not only stiffened her spine more than the wall at her back but also her resolve. He loved watching the fire grow in her gaze. "I would dare quibble, with *you*, dear sir, over anything and everything if it would keep you here, with me."

Her gaze flitted away from him and then returned, the unending ocean no match for the depths of emotion surfacing from her now.

"For I confess, I did not know until you, until today, how so *very* much I have longed for a family of my own. A d-dream stifled, buried, under duty and responsibility. All but for-g-gotten." She was crying now, near-silent tears that shook her lips and clawed at his chest. He could damn near taste the salt on his own thickened lips as he watched the stray droplets slip unheeded down her face. "I am both in alt and dismay at how this"—her fingernails scored his scalp —"you, have come to be. Here. W-with me."

"Liv. Olivia. Do not break my heart further with your sorrow, not now that it feels complete for the first time since— Since... In *ever*, I vow."

"Nathaniel." Again, her husky tone stroking the syllables in his name reached into the strangling trousers and cupped his ballocks, primed his prick beyond anything he'd known.

"Olivia, soon to be *Mrs. Oliver.*" He glared at her when she started to open her mouth, unwilling to allow another word of protest between them. A single shake of his head and she demurely closed her lips and gave a slight nod. "My turn?"

"Please." Her small smile was tremulous, but it was a smile. A welcome one.

"I cannot imagine confessing this to another," he scraped out as one of her hands slipped down to clasp his at her waist, the other fingered over his short beard. "Know that, if you think to doubt again."

After a single, audible inhale for courage, a harsh exhale for delay, he wasted not a moment more. "My one profound regret is that I did not value Ellen more, that I wasn't home when she breathed her last. But do you not see? Olivia, you, *you* promise to be my staggering joy. You and only you."

Nerve-riddled seconds elapsed as she stared at him, as his heart thundered, pounding against his ribs as though to burst free. "Olivia, please. Do not force either of us to regret not grabbing on with both hands to this wondrous chance life—and wily Hastings—has given us."

Her lips mashed together, eyelids came down, another three blasted tears squeezed free before she fluttered open glistening lashes and whispered, "Forgive me. I regretted sending you away the moment you were gone."

"And I regretted leaving, had already turned around *before* encountering Hastings."

"Nathaniel..." That sweet sigh did it.

He kissed her, claimed her in a hard, fierce, fast action that had both their tongues dueling, lips probing and hands grasping before he released her mouth, his jagged breath a rasp between them.

He hauled her back into his arms and swung for

the bed. "Now let me tend your leg, will you? With all due haste. Because if we don't soon finish what we started this afternoon, I vow..."

She plopped gently down on the mattress, legs hanging off the side. "Vow what?"

*So many things.* But 'twas time to play nursemaid... "'Tis dark as a cave in here."

Now that he *needed* to see, to take care of her, the lack of light frustrated. He reached for the single, unlit taper near her bed and frowned at it.

"I had a lamp," she said weakly, "but it ran out of oil. There are more candles downstairs. I think. Maybe?"

"I only need the one for what I'm after." He brought the small table closer, cursing when he realized one of the legs was cracked. "Not about to put a live flame on that."

So he dragged her sturdy trunk over, wincing when he bumped into the full pail and water sloshed over the side. "Charming place you have here."

"It's falling apart, I know," she groaned, restless fingers rumpling her skirt above her knee. He noticed how she avoided looking at her injuries. Hmm. When it came to her own discomfort, was his redoubtable Olivia *squeamish*? "Has been since we moved in."

"Structurally, it's sound. I noted the foundation on my first walk of the perimeter before I took up the gardener's position. Wait here. I'll get this lit and—"

"Miss 'Ales?" A scratch on the door followed the servant's gravel-voiced call. "'Ave supplies, I do."

"Ensuring I haven't had my wicked way with you,

more like," Nate muttered, crossing to the door. Which he opened and swung wide, to show Olivia in her seated, still-attired glory.

He commanded the small tray the servant brandished, taking care with the lit candle. "Thank you for this. As you can see, your mistress is safe."

The man ignored him and angled toward her. "Miss 'Ales?"

"Captain Oliver is correct, I am safe with him. Thank you for checking, though. Jacks? Please, mmm"—for the first time, her voice lost its composed quality with the fellow—"um, please—"

"Do not interrupt again," Nate finished for her, glaring at the "helpful" servant.

"Miss?" And like any good employee should, the man completely ignored Nate and looked to Olivia for confirmation.

"We-might-be-a-bit," she said in a rush of words. "So, aye, please await our return downstairs."

Aiming a scowl at Nate, the man nodded once and departed, grumbling beneath his breath about the crazed weather stirring up cracks in more than just the cursed house.

Shutting out the disturbance, Nate latched the door, a rebellious thrill flaring through him when he engaged the working lock. Next, he inventoried the arrival of bandages and cloths, the bowl of clean water and the appreciated candle, which he used to light the other.

"He's all bluster," she said.

"Not hardly." Securing both candles and tray

upon the trunk, he took up her hand and moved in betwixt her legs until he was kneeling before her. Giving her fingers a squeeze, he said, "You forget, I have seen your man in action. He knows how to defend his ladies."

"I keep telling you, *not* a lady."

At her words, he released her fingers and lightly tapped his over her mouth. "Not that again. You *are*, Liv. Mine. *My lady*, my woman. One with an injured limb and I think, perhaps, a wounded heart." He gave his eyebrows a quick wiggle which brought a surprised, bashful smile to her lips. And then she kissed his fingers before he slid them away. "And my goal is to heal both."

At her shy nod, he returned to her leg, noting how she still avoided looking at the torn stocking and skin she'd bared to his gaze. All right, then. Distractions, he could provide.

"Hurts, I know," he said, while removing her slipper and carefully peeling her ripped stocking down.

"Not as much as sending you away. I'm sorry for that. For how I behaved earlier. Well, not all of it, but —*you know*. How things ended. That is what I'm sorry for. *Not* the rest."

During her blather, he looked up to find her flushed gaze meeting his, the admission heating her cheeks in a way that warmed him all over. The stocking gone, her bare leg exposed, he placed one hand above her knee, stroked his palm over her unin-jured thigh. "Ah. Then let me fix that. Listen well."

She made a strangled sound in her throat, her leg quivering beneath his light touch.

"IF YOU WANTED TO RUIN ME," Olivia confessed, not ready to hear what else he might say. Could anything surpass what had come before? "You have succeeded." She'd never look at another man again, not after what they shared.

"Mayhap you don't have the right of it." His words were resolute, hard even, despite how his tender touch upon her upper leg worked magic upon the dull throb aching in the lower. "I am ruining you for *me*. I find that after having known you only a few short hours, that I need you in my life and I want you for my wife. Your smile. Your scent. Your kisses." His gaze flicked to her bosom. "Your breasts."

"For shame, Nathaniel..."

"Now that's what I wanted to hear. My name, in that alluring, breathy way of yours. That and *yes*."

"Yes?" Disbelief colored her tone, but she couldn't stop the growing hope spreading from her ears inward. Because that was twice now.

"Aye. Y-E-S, to everything henceforth."

Twice now: first a mention of marriage. And now wife. *He really meant it?* "Yes to what? I cannot recall any particular questions. Not coming my way, that is. Seems I have asked an inordinate amount of you today—a hundred or more—yet have received very little information in return."

"Promise I will take care of all that later. I have a

thousand and one things to tell you. Share with you. A lifetime's worth, in fact. But for now, *my* questions. Your answer to every one: *Yes*."

"Still waiting to learn, my answers to...*what*?"

"*Yes, Nate,* I want to marry you." She sucked in a breath at having it confirmed, and so very decisively. Releasing her thigh with a rousing squeeze, he saturated one of the cloths and began washing her leg.

While he worked, she focused on the strength of him, kneeling before her, where he'd nudged her healthy leg aside while propping her other foot upon his cocked knee. How he concentrated on her with more intensity than she'd yet to experience from another. She, diffident, usually invisible "Wivy" was *seen* by this man, made bolder and more confident by his view of her. How it boggled.

"*Yes, Nate,* is how you shall respond," he ordered, this time with a wink, as he pried free a large sliver that had her eyes swimming both with pain and relief —and mayhap wonder, too, when he bent to kiss above the area now soaking a small cloth with fresh blood.

Quickly did she wrench her attention back to his face, where the candles' twin flames danced golden upon his bristled cheek and jaw. "*Yes, Nate,*" he instructed once more, "I cannot wait to mother your fiendishly splendid daughters. *Yes, Nate,* I might not mind having one or two of my own, with you—with *me,* that is." He flashed her a grin and went back to binding a long bandage around the wound. "*Yes, Nate,* I want to grow old with you. To laugh with you, to love you (I'm willing to gamble this one will come in time)—even if you don't command twenty-seven trillion pounds to your name."

"'Twas twenty-seven *zeros*, I believe." 'Twas a squeak, is what it was, when he tied off the bandage with a grunt of satisfaction, leaving it comfortably snug around her calf.

At that impertinent correction, his eyes glinted. "*Yes, Nate*, whatever you ask, even if you cannot recall how many zeros you lack in your accounts."

Olivia laughed. "Are you intending to persist through the night, until I give you every answer you want?"

"*Yes, Nate*," he continued, as she stared into the expressive, stormy slate of his gaze, he rose to standing, a strong and powerful presence before her. "I realize this is the very pinnacle of daft and not what either of us thought we wanted when we woke this morn, but I cannot abide the thought of waking again without you by my side. *Yes, Nate*—"

She silenced him by placing one trembling finger against his lips. "Of course, yes. *Yes*, you baffling, buffle-headed man."

He kissed the finger residing against his mouth, then shackled her wrist and pulled it away, continuing in a more subdued tone as he crowded closer, where she sat upon the bed. "*Yes, Nate*, I shall move in with you, or you with me, whether it be the leaking, lightning-singed stables or the loud and crowded abode of your sister's. I will contentedly live with you and yours until we can find another home to call our own. *Yes, Nate...*" After a three-second pause, he flashed her a rueful grin. "It appears I'm out—but only for the moment, mind. Olivia? I didn't imagine that 'yes' I thought I heard in there, did I?"

"You didn't," she assured him, the wheels in her mind turning faster than those on a runaway carriage.

"Then what is that speculative gleam in your eye? You're not already thinking of ways to jilt me, are you? Lest you forget, I have a *long*-standing personal acquaintance with a certain vicar, who just happens to be waiting downstairs, and if I must, I shall claim *you* carried me up here only to have your wanton way with me."

"I have an idea. A wild notion to be sure, but hear me out?"

"Wilder than this—us? Becoming smitten in less than a full day? I am all aghast." He nuzzled the skin beneath her ear. "Speak on, dear one. It seems my formerly predictable existence has been flipped topsy-turvy and I find I don't mind a jot."

"Aside from that herd of notable zeros, are your moderate pockets sufficient to..."

"To what? Sufficiently deep? I'd say so, when I'm not wearing *these* blasted trousers."

"Yes, well, I happen to adore these particular trousers, so don't go consigning them into rags quite yet. You said you liked this house. Did you mean it?"

"Aye. It's like an old Gothic castle, a miniature one to be sure and without the moat but what—" He must have read her thoughts, that or her expression conveyed the idea. "Buy *this* place? Is that what you're thinking?" At her nod, he straightened and turned his gaze upward, his eyes surveying the perimeter of the ceiling, the drizzle lining one wall, the disintegrating wallpaper beneath, even the ratty remains of a small rug she'd hung over a chair to dry. He looked like a little boy when he grinned. "Would your lady be amenable to selling, do you think?"

"Would your daughters like it here?" *Would you?*

"I daresay they'd adore it. Hope loves spending time outside and digging in gardens every bit as much as I do and the peeling plum wallpaper alone would garner her undying appreciation. Everything at Susanna's is elegant, 'beyond bearing for more than a few hours' or so Charity claims, far too perfect that she's afraid of messing something up. And Faith? She's my adventuress. She'd love nothing more than exploring beneath every rotted board and behind every chipped stone."

"But what about *you*?" She insisted on knowing.

"Me? I'm not afraid of hard work when it's for something, some*one* I value." He gestured toward her wrapped leg. "Why did you not paint an X upon them?"

"Upon what? My *legs*?"

"The weak boards. Until they could be repaired."

Oh. That was rather clever. "Because you were not here to suggest it?"

"Say things like that and they will go to my head. Now come. I am sure that leg is aching, so sit with me while I endeavor to steal your attention away from it."

"Oh ho." That playful, flirty side of herself that

had been absent until meeting him roared back to the surface. "And how might you intend to do that, dear sir?"

"Minx."

Sitting on the side of the bed closest to the trunk where he adjusted the taper, he tugged her into his arms and pulled forth the sealed letter Hastings had given them downstairs. "This. Are you not curious?"

In answer, she settled against him, thrilling at his warmth behind her and below her as he tugged her fully into his embrace, arms around her middle, anchoring her firm upon his lap as he gave the letter over into her care.

# 17

# A LETTER AND A BIT OF LONGING (YO, FISHIES!)

*Should things be looking grim:*
*Give to the lady in question if all else*
*should fail.*

"ARE THEY?" she queried upon reading what was scratched—elegantly so—upon the outside of the folded square. "Looking grim? I would have claimed the opposite."

"True." He stroked one of his hands down her arm and laced their fingers, pulling her hand over her shoulder and bringing the back of it to his mouth. Where his tongue did delightfully naughty things to the skin there. After several seconds where her stomach soared and heart threatened to match it in elevation, his lips released her with a small *smack* of suction. "Nevertheless, I admit to exceeding curiosity." Brushing his thumb over the dampened area, he returned her hand to the other—and the shaking letter in her weakened grasp. "So, we shall read it together."

She jerked to the side so she could see his face. "You know not what's inside?"

"Have not an inkling."

"Well then. Shall we appease our joint curiosity?"

He ran one finger down the side of her face, from her temple past her cheek, over her jaw and her neck, whispering hotly into her ear, "That is not all I hope to appease, so please read swiftly, my lady."

Aglow from his unspoken promise, Olivia ran her finger beneath the seal and unfolded the first crease, only to be met with additional guidance before the letter itself was revealed:

*Aye, you hold in your hand the ramblings of a Fallen Woman. Should you refrain from casting this straight into the fire, I would guide you in your decision...*

An indrawn breath, full of gasped surprise, next to her ear told Olivia they likely read apace.

"Well now," Nate whispered, his chin resting upon her shoulder, "'twas not expecting anything of that sort. Go on, now. I know we are both in alt for the rest."

Trembling fingers unfolded two more creases and then the full letter came into view.

*March 4th, 1815*

*Dearest Lady Scandal,*

*I applaud your bravery for enlisting such an advertisement to secure a spouse. I hope you I pray you are successful beyond Your wildest imaginings. If you are reading this, you have hesitations about accepting the suit of Nathaniel Oliver.*

*Granted, I may not be privy to his financial accounts, but I doubt he has the full extent of funds you need, based on your stipulations. Yet I would encourage you, strongly, to consider what he does have to offer. To consider him as spouse.*

*While I freely admit I am not his mistress, nor have I ever been, I have been mistress to many.*

*My occupation, if you will, has taught me how to recognize the quality of a man.*

*To know that some who may be exquisite in intimate matters, may not be honest in others. To learn that while some may be generous with their purse—and physical attributes—they may not be generous of themselves. Their heart, my lady; it may forever remain locked.*

*I do not believe that would ever be the case with Nate Capt. Oliver. From what I have observed*

*over the years, with how he treated Ellen Eliza-
beth, from my admittedly distant yet experienced
view, he proved a steadfast, dedicated mate to her
from beginning to end.*

*A single time, long ago, prior to a youthful
Nathaniel sailing off, but after their vows were
said, I offered advice on how to safely partake of the
pleasures to be had in ports abroad (to prevent him
from returning with anything injurious to himself
and thereby also to El, his wife at that time).*

*To my delighted dismay, he quite vehemently
insisted my counsel was unneeded.*

*I do believe, my brave Lady Scandal, you have
before you now a man who was true to his wife.
True to his vows. What a rarity! (And yes, I
should know.)*

*If you find any accord with him at all, any passion
you are curious to explore, I bid you to consider his
suit with all earnestness and patience. Assuming,
that is, that you possess the patience to raise his
three daughters. To mother them as though they
were your own.*

*Whether you enlist the aid of a qualified, genteel
governess—one who would rule without the
whip—*

"Without the *whip*?" Nate muttered over her shoulder just as her eyes happened across the same line, echoing her aghastment. "Good God. More to their pasts than I knew..."

*Their?* she wondered.

*—or whether you are bold enough to take that task on yourself, ensure that his daughters are educated in ways that will benefit them as they must one day care for themselves and hold their own in future. If you have any interest in a family, there can be no better one in my stark and honest opinion than the charity, hope and faith (along with Charity, Hope and Faith) that Nathaniel A. Oliver would bring to any union.*

*If you do marry into the family, I would delight in meeting you at some future time.*

*Yours in brazen activities (and in confidence, one must hope),*

*Always,*

*–S*

Olivia ran the flat of her palm over the elegant script, smoothing the creases. Breaths coming oddly fast, she scooted to the side, off his lap so she could read his expression. "You know who troubled themselves to send this? The Brazen Miss 'S'? But are surprised by it, nevertheless, aye?"

More than half expecting him to deny any knowledge of a self-admitted mistress, regardless of whether they had been intimate or not, she was still taken aback by how pale he'd become above the dark stubble of his beard.

Shaking his head, he cupped one palm over his lips, staring hard at the sheet she held.

After several seconds of silence, the color slowly began to leach back into his face as he lowered his hand to whisper. "I know. It can be none other, but... I confess... I am more than a little dumbfounded. By her note. Her confessions. The realities of which I had remained ignorant until moments ago...

"But the play on the girls' names reminds me of something Ellen would have said, which only confirms...

"Sarah is El's older sister. She has always resided and worked in London, even since before El and I wed. But our mysterious 'S' can be none other." He whistled. "That comes unexpectedly. Sarah is not the sort one would expect... I mean, when one thinks of mistresses and courtesans, does one not think...I don't know...*beyond* elegant? Stunningly beautiful? Tall and composed? Not that Sarah isn't those things, but, well...she isn't." He gave a reluctant shrug and looked as though he experienced guilt simply uttering such things. "She's an inch or two above average height, but nothing overly impressive. Is passably pretty but not what men think of as smashing, in fact Ellen used to complain her sister had turned into something of a dowd—"

"Do you not think perhaps she subdued her charms? Intentionally, when she came to visit?"

"You're brilliant, Liv. That's exactly the sort of thing she would do." After a deep inhale and exhale, a grin tilted one half of his mouth. He pointed to the letter in her hand. "As to that, I wonder if she heard of the ruse to marry me off from Susanna or one of the girls, decided to join in without invitation."

"And now you know her... Profession. Did you suspect before?"

"None of it. Not a hint." His voice slowly grew in volume as he caught her gaze, his looking both troubled and a bit impressed. "But she's always had a quiet fortitude, a strong confidence about her that commands respect despite her soft-spoken ways."

"Did Ellen, you think? Know about Sarah's true occupation?"

"Nay, she believed her sister to be the housekeeper-in-charge of a grand London townhome. I forget the lord whose name she mentioned, but I remember well how her letters were filled with anecdotes that oft had us all laughing.

"The gifts she lavished on us all each Christmas and at birthdays. Her reticence to visit more than once or twice a year.

"But this explains much." He reached around her back and hugged her to his side. "So much, I am thinking. It would be like Sarah to sacrifice herself, if she thought it would help save her sister. Ellen was never robust, not even when we met, but she was healthy enough.

"It wasn't until after Faith was born we noticed anything amiss. But each visit home brought the truth, she was growing weaker in body if not in spirit. After reading that"—he gestured toward the note she'd refolded and placed slightly beneath the tray—"so much makes sense. Right before I met El, she claimed her parents and brother had died. Influenza. And her sister had just started working in London. I wonder now how much was simply happen-so between us. Whether her parents had really *just* died or if Ellen and Sarah were perhaps on their own longer than I knew, with the elder Sarah protecting her younger sister."

The doubts seemed to buffet him like a fierce wind. His lips compressed, as he shook his head in denial, and her heart ached for the young man he'd been, perhaps naive, and now uncertain.

A determined glint filled his gaze. "Despite what we have just learned about Sarah, I am choosing to believe what I knew of Ellen was truth. I cannot start questioning everything now, not with the girls still grieving her loss. Since Ellen decided upon their first names, she encouraged me to choose their second: Charity Jane, Faith Anne and Hope Everlasting. I—"

"You *didn't*! Nate, tell me you did not burden Hope with 'Everlasting' as—"

He chuckled. "Hope *Elizabeth*, after her mother— you just had such a rapt look on your face, I needed to confirm you were listening. Truly wanted to hear all this."

*Always.* "Always will I take joy in hearing any tales of your past. Be they tinged with sorrow or joy. Never doubt that."

"Giving Hope part of her name seemed paramount. Because I sensed she'd be Ellen's last. My last. For we both knew by then her body wouldn't sustain carrying another child.

"But now... Who knows what *our* future together may bring about? Whether it's six cats, fourteen rabbits and a hedgehog; whether it's a flock of grandchildren compliments of the virtues in fifteen or twenty years, or possibly a son or daughter of our own, Olivia, I care not. I only know I must spend those years with you."

Choosing to forgo any attempt at grace, she rose to her knees, shoved his chest backward until he landed upon the mattress and swung one leg over his thighs. "You have me," she promised, finally surrendering to the inevitable conclusion since she'd stumbled across him in the garden. "And whether it's doubts or dreams, regrets or fond remembrances, please share them with me. Ellen shaped both you and your daughters, and I would know her through you. And if she *did* happen to deceive you at the beginning?" Her fingers clenched in the fabric of his shirt, as her shoulders lifted and a feeling of embarrassed chagrin heated her cheeks. "Then may I only hope she and I make good company for each other, and for you?"

He plucked one of her hands free from his shirt and intertwined their fingers to bring the underside of her wrist to his lips. "Deceit, eh?" He smiled against her skin. "Regardless, she was a good mother, and Sarah has been a wonderful aunt."

"Will you let Sarah continue to visit? Now that you know?"

"How she earns her living? Would you? Were you their mother?"

Was he truly curious what she thought about entertaining a "fallen woman"? Or did he prefer one response over the other? It mattered not, for her answer came swiftly. "Absolutely, she would be welcome. That letter writer entrusted me—er, Lady Scandal—with a confidence that could ruin not only her, but her relationship with her nieces and her brother-in-law. And she risked all to speak in *your* favor. Aye, she will be welcome."

A single nod of agreement betwixt them and the matter was closed.

DOWNSTAIRS, Mathias Trumbull (usually only known, referred to, or addressed as "Vicar" no matter that he possessed a decent-enough name) sat upon a rickety bench, pretending to nibble at the worst scone this side of hell and glared at his uncle.

"What have you not been telling me? This entire outing, I vow, is fraught with lies and deception. I am sure of it."

Uncle Bamber just smiled, the sly, crafty quirk of his lips only family was privy to. His elderly relation —spryer than one might think given his years—took a small, very small, sip of the worst tea on planet Earth (Mathias knew, having already discarded his out the largest chink in the boarded window as soon as the footman had stepped away). "Why, Nephew, whatever could you mean?"

Ah. Prevarication. Do not tell an untruth to the vicar. Keep him in the dark (much like this room they'd been shown to) rather than risk telling an outright lie to a man of God. Thias gave his uncle a piercing look, flicking a scone crumb his direction. "Do you seek to salvage your worldly conscience with your lies this day by pretending ignorance?"

"*My* conscience?" Old blue eyes sparkled. "Nay, Mathias. Mayhap I seek to salvage your moral one."

The muscles in his stomach clamped. This time with hunger and not in revolt of that first—and only —full bite of sinfully salt-laden scone. He grunted. How to get his uncommunicative uncle to share what he needed to hear, to at least calm the churning in his soul, if not his gut.

"Does Aunt Margaret know?" Thias gestured to the rooms above where the occasional laugh, or thump (or squeal or whimper), made things clearer than a man of the cloth might wish. Thick walls and ceilings were all well and good but did not do a farthing when sound traveled through the cracks of open windows. "What machinations have you contrived to bring about this day?"

"Nephew. Thou woundest me." Aged hands clasped to his chest in the most overly dramatic of manner, his uncle recited, "*Machinations, hollowness, treachery, and all ruinous disorders follow us disquietly to our graves.*" Then his uncle straightened and all but winked. "Trust, Nephew. Unlike so many in Shakespeare's beautiful tragedy, Maggie Mae and I have no yen to see our graves early. Why would we be involved in anything of a nefarious nature? Be assured, we are as innocent as lambs."

"Wolves dressed as lambs, mayhap."

Uncle Bamber only laughed.

A distant if unmistakable moan found its way to his ears, and Thias's throat made a strangled sound of dismay and disbelief. An unholy grunt, one might say.

For a man celibate for many years, after sowing early-age oats, he could at least give thanks that more than his manly "staff" had settled into life as a minister. His heart may finally have embraced, at least in part, the calling that was thrust upon him by birth order and little else, but that did not mean he didn't long for a woman—a wife—of his own. Especially when a few more groin-stirring, breathy moans floated in from the direction of the boarded window behind them.

Now more than his stomach clenched.

"Your aunt knows every bit of what goes on."

"Somehow, I doubt that," Thias muttered.

His uncle shifted, rose and stretched each leg before circling the room twice ere he resumed his seat. "She does. I keep no secrets from my dear Maggie Mae. In fact, 'twas her suggestion I ask you accompany me today."

And he would have to be content with that, if not his own situation, given how Uncle resumed his place at the long bench across the giant slab of a table and proceeded to feign a doze.

Time elapsed.

The hour grew late. Then later still.

The burly footman returned with more weak tea and a single candle before making excuses and disappearing back from whence he came.

After some while, seeing Uncle fidget more than once, Thias spoke again. "I do have a sermon to work on. Cannot linger *all* night here." They would already be making most of the journey to Duffield in full dark.

"You are *always* working on a sermon," his uncle said rather accurately, rising to stretch his joints around the room again. "Worry not about this eve. You will stay the night upon our return. Your aunt will feed us both. Come fishing with me tomorrow, before you travel on to the vicarage? Practice your sermon on me and the fellows with fins. We can work on it together."

His conscience battled his duty. Duty to the law, to the church, the banns. To his oath. To the joyfully sinning couples above—if their sounds were anything to go by. "One hour more. Then we must leave."

"Three," Uncle insisted, "and I shall see you have

a full loaf of your aunt Margaret's gingered bread come Sunday."

"*Two* loaves," Thias countered. "And two hours."

*Weak, man. Your values bought by bread?*

Nay, his sense of happiness buffered by love. For if he didn't miss his guess, his crusty old uncle had turned to the business of matchmaking in his older years, and did the Good Book not speak highly of having a mate?

*And they were both naked, the man and his wife, and were not ashamed.*

Argh. And why did he have to go and think of *that* verse?

Would that *he* could find the one whom his soul could love...

BAMBER HASTINGS, stamming fine solicitor that he was, glanced over at his long-suffering nephew. The sigh that had escaped the man was loud enough to have been heard past heaven's pearly gates, not to mention by an old, mischievous crank scheming to make those around him happy and married—preferably happily married.

Had he not given Mathias decades to find his own woman?

He had. And with more patience than most.

Does the Lord not say, *It is not good that man shall be alone?* He did indeed say that. Therefore, Bamber thought, eyeing his nephew by marriage, I shall find a helpmeet for *him.*

Heh. Heh.

'Twould make his own beloved beyond happy if her favorite nephew had someone to share his pillow. His table. His flock.

Bamber knew his Maggie Mae had questioned the marbles in his garret, given the amount of time he had spent working toward arranging just the right order of applicants for Lady Scandal to interview.

A distant squeal and a laugh met his gloating ears (he ignored Mathias's flinch and chose to gloat some more, allowing an audible murmur of contentment to rise up from his chest).

He had, by damn—pardon, Sir (or Madam) Above —had indeed selected the right candidates and more importantly, put them in the right order. With the Great Lord's assistance, Bamber had seen to the blessed futures of the two ladies, their men, and even the trio of delightful Oliver daughters in the process.

So 'twas only appropriate he would turn his stamming attention toward a mate for the boy. Though if Mathias heard himself described thus? As a mere lad? Poor fellow would choke on more than the piss-poor tea and briny scones.

But now that Bamber had become renowned throughout London (all of Great Britain, some might say) as the solicitor brazen enough to put forth the now-infamous Lady Scandal's advert? Why, business of all sorts had been flooding into his tiny, unassuming Duffield office.

Surely someone would cross his notice, someone perfect for the sometimes pious yet good-hearted man sitting stiff and cross-armed on the other side of the table.

*What about the fish?* a small part of him prompted. *The ones crowded about in the waters, just waiting for your hook?*

Bamber smiled. Wiped a single piece of scone-salt off the corner of his lip and rubbed it between his thumb and finger, his mouth anticipating the sweet, gingered bread his love would have made anticipating his return. The fish?

The fish would wait for him every weekend, every Tuesday and Friday as well, for Bamber had decided to expand his business into more matchmaking.

He would hire another solicitor or three, to work for him, to handle the plethora of exciting new business floating his way, while he...

While he took his Maggie Mae and fishing rods to the river every Tuesday; his new employees every Friday and taught them what he could (because only a devilish sort of man didn't know how to fish); and he would reserve those long weekends for his delightful great-grandchildren.

Ah, life was grand indeed.

# 18

## TO SEW A FINE SEAM (OR AT LEAST PLY A NEEDED NEEDLE)

———◦———

"THE VICAR!"

"What?" Nate said, brow puckered in mock severity as he lifted his head from the mattress and glanced over her shoulder. "Do not tell me you wish me to summon him here to watch?"

She giggled and slapped his strong chest. Giggled! Her. Responsible, oft solemn Olivia Hales had slackened her strict bearing to the point that laughter seemed close to the surface. What a delight. "Do not dare do such a thing! But I just now recalled—we have left him downstairs with—" One hand covered her mouth as she realized just how many of society's rules she had broken and blasted through today. She gasped. "Mr. Hastings!" The one person she could think of who might be every bit as serious as herself (or as she had been, prior to Nathaniel). "Whatever will he, will *they*—"

"'Tis of no import," Nate consoled, his strong hand warm beneath the skirt of her dress, where it nuzzled up one thigh and over her hinterlands. "The two are related. Hastings' nephew. From what I could gather, he thinks you and I simply had a tiff and Mr. Tanner and...and..."

"Juliet," she put in helpfully.

"Right. That theirs is simply a love thwarted by parents. He has no notion of the truth."

"That we have all met today?"

"Today? Nay, for I begin to think I have known you a thousand lifetimes."

She bit her lips against affirming the same. Too new to put into words, it was. The marvel of her *feelings*. Her ardent emotions toward this man and his unmet brood. But then those pesky maxims she'd lived by for years poked back in. "Regardless, we have left Mr. Hastings and a *vicar* downstairs. With nothing, no dinner, no drink—"

"Shhhh. I'm sure your brawny footman is seeing to them. But as to our waiting holy man, shall I invite him to say the words over us?" Shackling one wrist, he placed her palm over his heart. The steady thumps calmed her frantic breath, even as his firm grip on her flank threatened to rile it anew. "I will, you know. Without hesitation. Because here"—through his shirt, he pressed her fingers against his flesh—"in my soul, I know this is right. Us. Together. I can retrieve him right now, have him speak over us before we—"

"After." She reached for his nape with her other

hand, angled his head toward hers until their foreheads touched. "We can behave goose-headed *after*."

"And you will return with me, aye? Meet my girls? Be their mother and my wife?" The questions sounded as statements. As commitments.

"My heart is so full at the thought I fear I will burst. But will they not be disappointed? Expecting the grand Lady Scandal, of the lands and—"

"And the debts, lest you forget."

Above one storm-swept eye, she traced his dark brow, two tiny grey hairs amidst the thick black. "Is... This... Real?"

Relocating both his hands to her armpits, he hauled her up his body as though she weighed naught. Rolled over until her back met the mattress, came down upon her, resting on his elbows and settling his weight between her legs.

*Augustus certainly feels real.*

"As real as forever," he whispered against her lips before taking hers in a deep, hard kiss that went on... forever.

And then her disastrous day dress and mud-coated petticoat was half unfastened, half torn away; his blue shirt swiftly pulled over his head; despised tight-as-sin trousers discarded so they could sin in truth.

And nothing in her life had ever felt so heavenly.


NATE WRESTLED with kicking his boots off—not an easy task with his lips occupied with hers, his hands fumbling free of his borrowed sleeves so he could bring both palms to her glorious breasts. Flesh overflowing his fingers, he cupped and kneaded, oh how he needed, as he plumped one amazing mound and brought it to his lips, after a succulently sensuous trip down her chin...her pale, soft neck, inhaling lemons and roses with every breath, every lick...

Until he circled the puckered flesh around one nipple and brought his lips about the tip, to lave and then to suck.

"Aye," she moaned, arching off the bed and thrusting her breasts just where he wanted them—closer. "Harder, if you would."

Oh, would he.

Boots finally *thump-thumped* to the floor and a hurried tussle with his trousers until they too landed without care. "Too heavy for you?" he murmured against her skin, reluctant to halt his sensual assault.

Her knees widened, legs came up on either side, one cold foot caressed his flank. "That answer enough?"

He chuckled against her breast, kissing his way across the valley of her chest to suckle the other. "Your feet are a frozen affair, woman."

She rubbed both against him, ground her heels in while he started stroking his palms downward, mapping all of her curves. Pebbled skin met his questing fingers. "All of you feels chilled," he lifted his lips to say, seeking her gaze in the soft glow of the tapers.

She scratched several nails through his hair, palmed the back of his head when he rose above her. "That, dear sir, is what comes of afternoon traipsing about in the rain."

He gripped her hip, loving the full weight of her healthy flesh, gave a light jiggle and stared down at her seawater eyes, and then her flushed and beard-scratched breasts with their tongue-moistened tips and grinned. "I shall have to warm you posthaste. 'Tis a newly coined husband's duty, I am sure of it."

With restless abandon, she released her hold on his shoulder and head and her legs jerked. "Oh? Does Gus double as a warming pan, then?"

On his journey downward, he swiped two fingers over one nipple, causing her to cry out. Another light finger slap and she squealed. "Nate! Yow."

He brought her legs over his shoulders and settled in between her thighs, where her scent was thicker. Beyond enticing. She propped herself up on her elbows and licked swollen lips, eyes glassy and bright. "What are you—"

"No more 'Gus' references from you, female, not when we're in bed. Else"—he angled onto one elbow himself, ignoring how she'd stiffened beneath him once he climbed into place—"I will not do this..."

His thumb caressed downward to a fresh wash of moisture. Below him, she melted. Head fell back, hips wiggled and damn if her temperature didn't rise five degrees. He caressed upward, her wet heat coating his thumb, inviting more. So his fingers joined in, the pads of several stroking in soft circles through her outer flesh, delighting in their welcome. Spreading her glistening glaze all around, he sought out her nub, already tight and protruding, and leaned in to lick just as he slid one finger deep inside.

Her body clasped tight. Hot. Her mouth muttered something about rainy days and sunny seamen, about lightning and loneliness, about glory and Gus. Saucy wench. So when he added a second finger to her cleft, and another circle of his tongue, he stretched his other arm up and pushed one finger past her lips to give *her* something to suck on.

Which she did. With a moan and a whimper. A greater tilt to her hips. A lurch to her pelvis.

Her heady taste went straight to his head. His tongue lashed, fingers thrashed, and before he knew it, she crested on a barely muffled scream, her inner muscles clamping and convulsing around his fingers as the rest of her feminine flesh relaxed and released, coating his tongue, his chin in the sweet syrup of sex.

Delighting him with the bounty of well-pleasured woman.

He inhaled down to his blazing ballocks. Was there ever a taste so fine?

AIR PANTED through Olivia's nose. Lightning flashed down to her toes.

She sucked his finger deep in her mouth and delighted in the masculine feel of him.

Her core? That intimate, secret part of her that "proper" women were instructed never to touch nor even acknowledge? It rejoiced like a chorus of a thousand. Sensations sang through her as tiny pulses clasped him over and over.

Breathy with wonder, she released his finger to murmur, "Mmm. Nathaniel. Now, the rest, please."

For she knew there was more.

So much more this man could show her.

He climbed up her body, his light chest hairs grazing her breasts. The solid bulk of his weight upon her, divine.

"My lady?" He nibbled her chin before kissing her fully—giving her a taste of her flavor upon his mouth.

Her tongue sought his, the contact satisfying some craving deep within. But not all. "Hush now. If *Gus* isn't allowed in bed between us, I daresay *Lady* has no place either."

She pushed at his shoulders and rolled him to his back. Still shaking inside. Mayhap outside too. But she needed to see him, his face, this next time. *This first time.*

With ungainly grace, she straddled his torso, flinched when his protruding staff nudged her hinterlands, and then lifted and arched, moved to place him —*it*—in front of her.

*You've already touched it once.*

Holding his heated, heavy-lidded gaze, deeply aroused at the sight of his dark hair upon her dainty pillow, she reached for him, touched the familiar tip first, then slid her fingers down and tried to grip the rest.

"Awkward angle for that perhaps, Liv." His raspy whisper came between them.

*Liv.* No one had ever shortened her name thus. He'd used it several times this evening. Upon his lips? 'Twas a caress of its own.

He reached between them and circled the base, aimed his erection upward, making it easier to fondle.

"Pet or play," he fairly growled, "but do you not take me inside soon, your eager man is likely to spend and embarrass himself all over again." The fingers upon her thigh flexed. "Save me from that shame?"

She lifted onto her knees, nudged herself forward and sought out—

*Found. "Ahhhmm."*

He rubbed his tip between her legs, though she controlled how much went in. He hovered at her entrance and asked how she wanted him. All of him. As deeply as he could go.

Bracing her palms upon his chest, she circled, fit the head between swollen, passion-slick flesh and heard him gasp. Felt his cock strain upward.

And she came downward.

One slow, somewhat sloppy shift, and then a sigh. She slid downward...downward. Grunting at the fit. The fullness. The strain of muscles unused.

The glory of it. The utter perfection.

Her alcove met his abdomen, his waiting thumb which she nestled against *that spot* again.

His other hand gripped tight to her thigh. The sight of his dark fingers pressing in against her pale flesh, the look in his fiery slate gaze... The indescribable, growing ache where they met and joined...

Everything compelled Olivia to straighten her shoulders, arch her back and *move*.

To ride him as though his loins were her saddle.

Not controlled. Not smooth.

No grace nor finesse to her actions.

Knowing all of that would come in time, content to wait, to practice, she embraced the uncoordinated movements, the eager, unbridled jolts of her body around his. Clenching him harder, she came down over and into him as though it were a race. Yet she needed more—

As though in answer, he rubbed her flesh above where they were joined.

Her toes tingled. Lips and fingers went numb.

She ground herself into his hand, tiny whimpers escaping her lips. Her hips flailed as she thrashed, the sensations streaking deeper, running hotter... Then bursting into such relief, she fell upon his chest, crying. Gasping.


Nate went rigid. Seconds from release.

His tensed hands went to her shoulders. "Liv? What is it? Did I hurt—"

Shaking fingers scrambled to cover his lips, to cup his face; elbows propped on his chest when she sought his gaze even as his hips jerked without restraint, his damn poker snug within her clasping sheath.

Moisture clung to her lashes. "No, nay. Beautiful. Wondrous. Only just recognizing my own staggering joy. Carry on."

Her salty tears upon his smiling lips, he did.

Wrapping his arms tightly around her back, fingers tangled within her unfashionably long hair, he held her to his heart and thrust upward. Frisked into her receptive, welcoming body. Unleashed the fury of his desire as he hadn't *in years*.

His arms contracted. Heart expanded. And mouth sought and claimed hers as he swived into his own lady until, only a few strokes more, release thundered between them.

THE SWEAT SURPRISED HER.

Never having thought about it, Olivia didn't realize how much heat two slick and naked bodies would create. And to think, mere hours ago, she was chilled so far to the bone, she thought her heart had turned to ice.

Cuddled alongside Nate's rugged, abused body, her head propped on one bent arm, she draped the other across his battered chest, reveling in the loose grip of his strong fingers along her forearm, where they had come to rest. Sheened with perspiration, somewhat mortified by the wetness betwixt her thighs, but still marveling in that too, she was surprisingly content to remain there forever. In her forlorn, leaking room with the day's humidity and the arms of her lover (how wondrous, that!) surrounding her.

"I am sure there exists no reason to say it, but I shall. Both as I know you value honesty, but even more to mitigate the guilt that hovered all day since I first failed to correct your misassumption in the garden." She had to swallow twice before continuing. "I am not an experienced widow. Not anything close to the landed lady who placed the advertisement."

"I know." His fingers tapped idly against her forearm, his other hand firm against her flank. "Realized it on the soggy ride home. Took me a piece to puzzle out the conundrum between you and the real Lady Scandal. Your sister? Niece? *Aunt?*"

Sufficiently confident to finally relax, Olivia laughed. "Aunt? How old do you think she is? Nay, Juliet is my charge. *Former* charge. Her father married her off woefully young. I accompanied her, a servant-slash-companion of sorts. Over the years, a true friendship grew but *she* is the lady."

A sigh of resignation puffed through her lips. "While I am sharing, I might as well tell you everything. My mother was a seamstress; father a tailor with an eye toward learning, which served me well. No lofty pedigree, should that be what you seek."

"Did you inherit any of their talents with thread and needle? Should you be able to fit my form better than Susanna, I shall count myself the most fortunate of men."

"I'm a fair seamstress. When time and materials allow." She leaned over and kissed one of the dark splotches of pain he'd endured, forever buried beneath his skin. "Does it hurt you still?"

"Not anymore. Never will again, now that it's known the balm of your touch."

"Poetic..." she teased. "Something I would delight in listening to forever, your words. Your voice."

"Then listen well. I care not how nonsensical the speed of things may seem—mayhap this house *is* cursed or haunted—"

"Or blessed or charmed?"

"Aye. You have the right of it. Look at Tanner and your lady. Still ensconced together—even now."

"Look at you and me."

"So you fully admit it, then? That we are a match? One with a splendid future."

"I have only hesitated to do so for the fear of having happiness snatched ruthlessly from my ephemeral grasp."

"Do I feel a phantom? A ghost to you?" He splayed her palm against his beating heart.

"Nay. You feel hard and hot and muscular and inviting, and I hope you never stop holding me."

"Then we are of accord? A future it will be?"

"Between you and I?" Beneath her hand, his heart thumped solid and sure, confirming the single nod he gave her. "And your daughters. And what if another should come along?"

"Another...child?"

Olivia flexed her fingers, petted his chest. "Something we both should have thought of earlier."

"I did." He allowed his smile to widen. "For I already knew I was not letting you go."

"That certain of me, were you?"

"Nay. That certain of myself. Nothing in my life, save the ocean has ever struck me as completely as one glance from your briny eyes."

"Briny? Is that supposed to be some sort of ill-begotten compliment?" She considered a moment. "I have ugly saltwater eyes?"

He just grinned. "To me? Briny is the most beauteous sight in the world. I look into your eyes and my soul is soothed in a way I never thought to know."

"There! Did I not tell you that you were poetic?"

His fingers left her Lowlands to delve gently through her tangled hair. "Before we babble on till morn, I need you to ply your talents posthaste. Grab a candle, Liv. Trim the wick and light it anew, if you will. You're about to see just how high of esteem I hold you in."

"Oh?"

"Aye." He rolled over onto his stomach, away from her, taking the sheet with him.

"You scoundrel!" She tugged, but he held firm, keeping it anchored beneath his hips, leaving her sweat-dampened, lovemaking-glowing self exposed. If she could see better in their dim, private world, she'd vow his cheeks turned ruddy. "You baffle me. Why claim modesty now?"

"Wifely duty, I fear." He rose to his elbows and

spoke to the wall, avoiding her curious gaze. "Splinter, Liv. Right cheek. It's been plaguing me for hours. Be a love and dig, pull or burn it out. Please?"

Swiftly enough he didn't complain (much), yet slowly enough she was able to explore (though not as much as she wished), Olivia managed to oust the stubborn splinter.

Two, in fact, one embedded deep enough to draw blood upon its exit.

A low whistle escaped past Nate's lips. "Relieved that's over." Shuddering, he reclined back and reached for her. A kiss and a mock growl followed by, "Now get dressed, woman. For we have a vicar to stand proudly in front of—no blushing nor stammering, mind—and then I have something to show you."

She cast his revealed form an arch look, her cheeks heating. "Something *other* than your splinter-riddled hindquarters?"

He grinned. "I should say so. That calico you thought Henry was ignoring? Not a bit. Henrietta's had a litter of seven and I—"

"Henrietta?"

He chuckled, angling one shoulder off the bed and blindly reaching for his trousers. "I guess your stable boy came up with the name— What in blazes?"

His hand came back in to view, holding a dripping, saturated bunch of fabric. The glower on his face the sort one might aim toward a nest of vipers.

"The bucket?" Olivia started laughing. Couldn't stop as the water cascaded from the material in a seconds-long, messy splash. "You—you dr-dropped your pants in the rain bucket? And you," she fairly cackled, cheeks plumping, heart singing, "with so very many well-fitting alternatives on hand."

# 19

## OCEANS OF JOY

WEARING naught but a sheet knotted securely about his hips, his boots and the borrowed chambray shirt, Nate exited Olivia's room holding a wriggling, protesting woman.

"I told you I could walk. You cannot carry me down the stairs."

He shushed her with a kiss, one with firm lips and eager tongue, until she moaned and her complaints finally waned. "Which one?"

About half the doors were shut, giving him no clue to which might be occupied. Meager moonlight filtered in from the open ones along one side, showing the cloudy, storm-studded day had given way to a clear night.

As he'd inspected the wrap on her lower leg, to ensure their bed sport hadn't dislodged his earlier efforts, they concluded 'twas time to wrest her lady and Tanner from whence they'd hid and all face—er, greet—their visitors below. "Did we not agree? No more dithering. Which is hers?"

Olivia pointed and Nate crossed down the poorly lit corridor, only one single sconce aglow, his boots thumping hollowly on the wooden floors, given the lack of rug, to pause in front of the door indicated. He smiled when a furry paw stretched out to hook claws into the tip of his boot. Olivia gave a yelp, as he jostled her to watch the feline's antics. "I have you."

All business now, he straightened, jiggled the wonderful weight in his arms and jerked his head toward the door. "Shall you gain their attention, or shall I?"

"Shhhush!" She blushed anew, then placed her hand upon the door. When her light taps and scratches went unheeded, Nate braced Olivia high against his chest and quickly freed one arm to bang on the door thrice before securing his hold beneath her legs once more. "I daresay they will hear that."

"Hush, you," she snickered, then sobered. "Juliet. I so regret disturbing you"—Liv spoke toward the ancient doorknob—"but we have visitors. More precisely, *you* have visitors."

"Guests? At this hour?"

"A vicar. He insists he must be on his way soon and he refuses to leave without seeing you."

"The *vicar*?" The feminine screech of surprise squeaked from behind the door.

"Arranged by Mr. Hastings," Olivia explained. "Come to perform a wedding, dare I hope?"

"Tell him we'll be down directly." The deep tones of Mr. Tanner responded.

A light breeze wafted between cracked boards of the room opposite, smelling of the day's trials. Reminding him of its joys as well.

Before either he or Olivia could comment on the singe, either literal or the figurative one that had scorched between them from the moment they met, the door opened and a flash of orange and white sped forth. A second after that, and much slower, the duo emerged, Tanner holding a slight form close to his chest and taking great care to avoid bumping anything against her bound foot. With riotous, mussed hair and crumpled clothing, they appeared every bit as disheveled as Nate feared he and Liv.

"Ho! We meet again." Despite the shadows, Tanner grinned at him, indicating the female each man currently carried. "And like this. Found your own lady?" Tanner's arms tightened, hauling the delicate woman in his arms closer to his chest. "For this one is claimed."

"Quite all right, Tanner, for aye, I have found my own." Nate jerked his arms to still Olivia's continued complaints that she could walk.

"There is a vicar below? Truly?" Tanner asked. "At this hour?"

"Aye," Nate confirmed, "one who desires an audience with you and...Lady *Scandal*, I presume?"

"Juliet, please." The flame-haired, delicate bundle in the other man's arms invited. "And you are?"

"Your rejected suitor twenty-five." He shifted,

leaned his back against the wall and brought Olivia's squirming lemon-floral self within nuzzling range. "Nathaniel Oliver. Earnest claimant for *this* female's hand."

Tanner sniffed. "Do I smell smoke?"

"Again?" the woman with him cried. But resignation, not alarm glazed her features. "What burnt?"

"The barn—" Olivia began.

"Stable," he corrected, then rushed to comfort. "But only the roof. And only part of it."

The lady closed her eyes and shook her head. Tanner's booted feet shifted loudly on the wooden floor. He bent to her ear and whispered, "Fear not. We can rebuild if you wish. And the flames are out." Quickly, he glanced at Nate to confirm.

"Absolutely. All of them. Thanks to the rain—"

"And your quick efforts," Olivia added.

He smiled at her. "*Our* efforts." Then spoke to Tanner. "And now that the lightning has moved on, I'm confident we won't get any new sparks to worry over."

With a hearty sigh, the lady fluttered open her lashes. "Then we shall not. Worry, that is. But why are you holding Wivy?"

"I— We— That is—" Tensing within his hold, his Liv made a strangled noise.

He pretended to drop her. Gratified at the loud yelp that cut off her nonsensical complaints. Gratified more when her loose grasp tightened around his neck. "Why do you sputter about, my love? Is it so hard to tell her?"

"Nate! I have commitments! I cannot just up and leave. Not—not—"

"We have found accord every bit as much as it appears you and Tanner have. It seems, my lady," he now addressed the grinning, scandalous wench wholly at ease in Tanner's brawny embrace, giving silent thanks with every word that she'd chosen Tanner and sent Liv to console him. "Your faithful companion—"

"I am not her dog," quipped Olivia with a twinkle that belied her frown.

"Heaven forfend," put in the lady.

"—is reluctant to leave your side, I do believe. Something quite necessary if she's to cherish my heart and mother my brood."

"Nate." At last, his armful melted against him. "But I cannot up and abandon Juliet, not without notice and planning and—"

"Wivy," Juliet said with a gentle air of strength and resolve, capturing attention and silencing protests with naught but the two syllables. She casually swung the bandaged foot between them. "Dearest Wivy, of course you can leave me. You will, in fact. Consider yourself *fired*. Released. No longer in my employ. No longer my companion."

Juliet's gaze drifted upward as though in thought. "Come to think on it, I have yet to pay you for three quarters or more, so there." Looking imminently satisfied now, Juliet sought first his gaze, then Olivia's, and the broken-legged sprite's cheeks flushed and eyes gloated. "There now. You have no home, no job and no reference."

Olivia licked trembling lips. "And you sound entirely too satisfied over news that would distress any sane servant."

Juliet reached for Olivia and Tanner took one step closer until the lady's fingers clasped those of Olivia's. "Not servant, dearest. And we both know that. Not for years. Heed Mr. Oliver's wishes and *consider* agreeing to them, my friend."

"I like this one," Nate told Tanner, who gave a satisfied nod.

Juliet glanced up to the quiet man, grinning indulgently at them all, but who had maintained his peace thus far. "Is Mr. Oliver—"

"Captain," Tanner corrected.

"Is *Captain* Oliver a quality sort?" she asked smoothly, as though barefoot, sheet-draped conversations in dark corridors were all the rage. "Did you two converse earlier? Sufficiently for you to make a confident assessment?"

The tall blond man gave a single nod. "We did. He is, I believe."

"Passed Mr. Hastings' exacting tests," Nate reminded them all. "Even if my 'application' was a hash of lies and embellishments."

Olivia and Juliet both spouted objections to that as a gauge, grumbling about several others who satisfied the requirements, and how that alone could not be counted much of a recommendation.

Nate's perplexed gaze found the other man's. "Tanner?"

Hard blue eyes narrowed. "I gather you have yet to be regaled with the travesties, poor habits and deplorable actions of those who came before us."

"The twenty-three others?"

"Quite so."

"Ahh…" Nate mused. "More than the brutish lout this morning wasn't up to par? At least not in the women's eyes?"

"Nor in yours or mine, had we been present and privy to their behavior. I daresay Hastings saved the best two candidates for last."

Nate caught on. "So they would recognize our value, after the dross that came before?"

"Something like that."

"Mr. Tanner! I am confident 'tis you I hear." Mr. Hastings' voice climbed the stairs. "My nephew grows impatient to ensure the well-being of Lady Letheridge. Assuage his worry, sir?"

"In a trice," Tanner called out. Then kissed the head of his flame-haired lady.

"You, too, Captain Oliver! And Jacks is keen to hear from Miss Hales as well."

"We're all *splendid*," the gift in his arms made known, quite loudly. Then, arms tight about his neck, she whispered in his ear, "Splendid, thanks to you."

LATER THAT EVENING, when everyone else was abed (Cook, Jacks, Jacob, Tanner and Juliet) or gone (Hastings and Vicar Trumbull), Olivia stood in the circle of Nate's arms, stomach grumbling the lack of dinner, but the rest of her sated beyond belief.

The stable was less humid than earlier, a cool middle-of-the-night breeze blowing in during those still moments before sunrise. That time of day when everything outside seems to hold its breath, waiting for the incandescent glow of the sun to begin stretching from its slumber and across the sky, gently waking inhabitants up for another busy day.

But that was for another few hundred breaths at least, time she could savor quietly with the man at her back. Her husband. Wonder of wonders. He tucked his chin over her shoulder, both of their attention fixed upon the tiny new furry family illuminated by the lamp they'd scrounged, burning low, both out of respect and to conserve fuel. "What did I tell you, Liv? He's a faithful sort after all."

Before them, tucked in the driest stall to be found, burrowed beneath straw and a few fabric scraps no doubt scrounged from the house, Henrietta the calico reclined on her side, five tiny bodies suckling and enduring her industrious tongue baths, while two more, eyes still closed, lolled about the orange-and-white fluffy legs of their father. Henry, ignoring what he'd begat, who stared up at them, glaring, more like —showing off those sharp canines—making sure they kept their distance while his missus tended their young.

"And Hope?" Olivia whispered, thinking of Nate's youngest she had yet to meet. "Do you think she will demand a kitten when she hears about them?"

"Hope? My youngest is not the one you need worry about." His warm breath caressed the side of her neck. "Faith is more likely to abscond with four or more, hide them in various pockets, parasols and lunch pails."

Olivia's heart swelled at the thought. She turned within his embrace. "I cannot believe we are here, now."

"Together. *Always*, henceforth."

She turned her head until her ear rested against his heart, listening to the steady sound, and nodded. "The thought of meeting your girls terrifies me."

"Shall I confess the thought of meeting Lady Scandal terrified me? When Hastings demanded I apologize *in person*, I did everything I could to wile my way out of it." His arms tightened around her waist, breath came out in a gusty sigh that screamed of relief. "Thank God both Hastings and He had other ideas.

"As to the girls, worry not. We shall take it one daughter at a time." The vibrations of his strong, sure voice both soothed her nervous soul and roused her tired body. "Lest you forget, Mrs. Olivia Oliver, they will be *thrilled*, one and all. For was not marrying me off their brilliant idea?"

AND IN FIVE MONTHS' time, after finalizing the purchase of the manor house and grounds where they first met, Nate took his family of five (and a half, with a babe due several months hence) to the ocean.

A pleasure jaunt, but with a serious detour to visit Ellen's gravesite with his wife and daughters, a chance to share their past with Liv—who promised to be their future.

A vacation, to celebrate not only his growing family, but also his contentment, his joy.

Who would have known the abounding solace he would find scraping old wallpaper while listening to all four of his girls laughing, and making messes and memories, in the kitchen and beyond? Stubborn, full-of-laughs-and-love Olivia had taken to mothering his brood faster than Faith's two kittens had to scratching the new curtains.

And if sadness had visited them all when Susanna lost her babe, then having her stay over the summer with them while she mourned had given *all* the women in his life a chance to bond. Even Sarah had come down from London, to mother his sister while she recovered.

Lips pressed tight in remembrance, eyes understandably damp at all that had transpired, both sorrows and joys filled his mind...

Thankfully, for all of them, the joys triumphed.

Savoring the last day of their trip, surprisingly ready to leave the coast and return to their home outside of Duffield, he willed the late afternoon descending sun to slow. To pause. So he could memorize forever the warmth blessing his face, his life, as he watched Faith and Hope digging in the sand to the sounds of laughter and splashes, watched the too-close-to-grown-up silhouette of Charity, looking so much like her mother, bending to trail fingers in the tide.

With his arms wrapped snug around Liv, who leaned against his chest as she, too, gazed out over the ocean, he threaded his fingers with the feminine ones of the blessing who had made all of this possible, Nate breathed in the salty, sea air, drawing this moment deep into his soul. He brought their clasped hands to his mouth and kissed the back of hers, a touch of lemon mixing in with the ocean.

His heart overflowed.

Peace and happiness assailed him with the enduring eternity of the waves washing in to shore.

# THE END

## Author's Note

Howdy. Thanks for reading!

Sure hope you had fun falling in love with Nate and Olivia.

But wait! We left Susanna grieving the death of her unborn child? Well, Miss Susanna has a number of secrets she has kept from her brother and nieces. Those will be revealed when she finds her true love in ***Lady Reckless Steals a Kiss*** to be released later this year.

Meanwhile, ready for more steamy regency fun?

My hottest stories are the **Roaring Rogues Regency Shifters**. Check out Maggie Award of Excellence finalist ***Ensnared by Innocence***.

If you prefer something a bit tamer, **Regency Christmas Kisses** might be just the thing; start with ***A Snowlit Christmas Kiss***.

And if you want something in the middle, try ***Mistress in the Making***, an extended-length novel full of humor, heat and heartwarming angst.

For more information on upcoming releases and all the cat and dog pics you might want, >^..^< sign up for my newsletter at larissalyons.com.

She's blind but determined. He's grumpy but protective. Together? Pure holiday magic.

*A Moonlit Christmas Kiss*

He needs to walk again. But he may need her more...

FREE 40,000 word preview ebook available at all retailers.

## MORE CHRISTMAS KISSES

*Rescued by a Christmas Kiss*

She's seeking shelter. He's hardened his heart. His cat just wants chin rubs.

## ROARING ROGUES REGENCY SHIFTERS

*Ensnared by Innocence*
STEAMY REGENCY SHAPESHIFTER

Maggie Award of Excellence Finalist

*Changing into a lion isn't all fur and games.*

A Regency lord battles his inner beast while helping an innocent miss, never dreaming how he'll come to care for the chit—nor how being near his world will deliver danger right to her doorstep.

*If Darcy had been a shape-shifting lion who thought about frisking—a lot...*

STANDALONE ~ HEA ~ 81,000-WORD NOVEL ~ BOOK 1 - ROARING ROGUES REGENCY SHIFTERS

### Deceived by Desire
STEAMY REGENCY SHAPESHIFTER

*Meet a Shakespeare-quoting shapeshifter who wants nothing to do with love...*

Cursed into the form of a lion without nightly sex, Lord Nash Hammond wants only two things— his liquor strong and smooth, and his wenches wild and willing. What he doesn't need is a virgin!

HEA ~ BOOK 2 – ROARING ROGUES REGENCY SHIFTERS ~ 97,000 WORDS

*Changing into a lion is all fun and growls—until it isn't.*

---

### Mistress in the Making

*A fun, emotionally satisfying, steamy tale told in three parts: Seductive Silence, Lusty Letters, and Daring Declarations.*

### *Seductive Silence, Part 1*
### FREE at all retailers

Lord Tremayne has a problem. He stammers like a fool—at least that's what he learned from his father's constant criticism and punishing hand. Daniel now hides his troubles by barely saying anything. But then he goes looking for a new mistress and finds a delightful young woman who makes him, of all people, want to spout poetry. He thought he had a problem before? Avoiding meaningless dinner prattle is nothing compared to the challenge of winning the heart of his new lady lust.

### *Lusty Letters, Part 2*

Thea's fascinating new protector has secrets—several. Hesitant to destroy her newfound circumstances, she stifles her longing to know everything about the powerfully built—and frustratingly quiet—Marquis. But then his naughty notes start to appear, full of humor and wit, and Thea realizes she's about to break the cardinal rule of mistressing—that of falling for her new protector. *Egad.*

### *Daring Declarations, Part 3*

An evening at the opera could prove Lord Tremayne's undoing when he and his lovely new paramour cross paths with his sister and brother-in-law. Introducing one's socially unacceptable strumpet to his stunned family is *never* done. But Daniel does it anyway. And it might just be the best decision he's ever made, for Thea's quickly become much more than a mistress— and it's time he told her so.

**Historicals by Larissa Lyons**

REGENCY CHRISTMAS KISSES

*A Snowlit Christmas Kiss*

*A Frosty Christmas Kiss**

*A Moonlit Christmas Kiss (preorder)*

*(expanded version of *Miss Isabella Thaws a Frosty Lord*)

MORE REGENCY CHRISTMAS KISSES

*Rescued by a Christmas Kiss*

ROARING ROGUES REGENCY SHIFTERS

*Ensnared by Innocence*

*Deceived by Desire*

*Tamed by Temptation (forthcoming)*

MISTRESS IN THE MAKING series (Complete)

*Seductive Silence*

*Lusty Letters*

*Daring Declarations*

*Mistress in the Making - Bundle*

FUN & SEXY REGENCY ROMANCE

*Lady Scandal*

*Lady Imposter*

*Lady Reckless Steals a Kiss (2024)*

———————◦———————

**Contemporaries by Larissa Lynx**

SEXY CONTEMPORARY ROMANCE

*Renegade Kisses*

*Starlight Seduction*

SHORT 'N' SUPER STEAMY

*A Heart for Adam…& Rick!*

*Braving Donovan's*

*No Guts, No 'Gasms*

POWER PLAYERS HOCKEY series

*My Two-Stud Stand**

*Her Three Studs**

*The Stud Takes a Stand (forthcoming)*

**Her Hockey Studs - print version*

Literary
Madness!

www.ingramcontent.com/pod-product-compliance
Lightning Source LLC
Chambersburg PA
CBHW061754190726
48289CB00007B/1948